Retreat From Love

Retreat From Love

by Colette

translated from the French

and with an Introduction by

MARGARET CROSLAND

C2X

THE BOBBS-MERRILL COMPANY, INC.

Indianapolis · New York

Acknowledgments

I should like to thank Dr. Marthe Lamy, friend of Colette, for help in the interpretation of certain words and phrases; Monsieur Jean Minjoz, Maire of Besançon; and Madame Maria-Catherine Boutterin, great-granddaughter of the family friend who acquired the house 'Casamène' (15 Chemin des Monts-Boucons, Besançon) after Colette had left it, for sending me information and a drawing.

NOTICE

For reasons which have nothing to do with literature, I have ceased to collaborate with Willy. The same readers who gave a favorable reception to our six . . . legitimate daughters, the four *Claudines* and the two *Minnes*, will, I hope, enjoy *Retreat from Love*, and will perhaps be ready to find in this book something of what they liked in the others.

COLETTE WILLY

Retreat From Love

Introduction

Colette's novel *La Retraite sentimentale*, its title adapted here as *Retreat from Love,* was published in 1907, when Colette was thirty-four. It has the same heroine as the four "Claudine" books, which were written in collaboration with her first husband, "Willy" (Henri Gauthier-Villars), in circumstances which may never be entirely clarified. After these early titles, which appeared at the rate of one each year from 1900 to 1903, she wrote *Minne* and *Les égarements de Minne,* which her husband would not permit her to sign, but in 1904 he allowed her to publish *Dialogues de bêtes* under the name of Colette Willy. The following year more dialogues appeared, and the year after that, 1906, Colette and Willy

1

separated. She then spent much of her time in the company of her friend "Missy," the Marquise de Belboeuf, and made her debut as a mime on the Paris stage.

Although she published nothing during the year of the separation, she did not stop writing. She revised and finished *La Retraite sentimentale,* which she had begun some time earlier at the converted farmhouse Willy had bought at Les Monts Boucons in the Jura, an isolated area at that time, although within reach of Besançon. This house, which incidentally still exists, is the "Casamène" of the novel, and Colette would spend many weeks alone there in the summer, while Willy would make occasional visits from Paris. It was here that she worked out a new life-style for herself.

Her marriage was already strained when she began the book, but she was not yet ready to write a full-length work without strong recollections of what her husband had taught her, and she invented no new characters. Claudine, her homosexual stepson, Marcel, her friend Annie, and various other acquaintances had already appeared in more than one book, and it could be assumed that readers would be pleased to encounter them again. Renaud, Claudine's older and idealized husband, is far away in a Swiss sanatorium although rarely absent from her thoughts.

The characters had only developed to a predictable extent from earlier books. The once-flirtatious Renaud has been converted (by Claudine) to an existence of devoted monogamy; Annie has become a despairing nymphomaniac; Marcel is the prey of creditors and blackmailers. How was Colette to take them through a winter together, far from civilization? Partly by using Willy's technique for salacious storytelling, making Annie relate the highlights of her amorous career, and partly by allowing herself, through Claudine, to indulge her own love of the countryside, which had remained tangential to the story in the early books. By the end of the novel, people have been eliminated from the world of Claudine-Colette, and although the heroine senses that they will eventually return, for the time being, animals, flowers, trees, insects are more important to her; these represent life, love, happiness.

Retreat from Love reveals Colette at a moment of transition, still using material and techniques which were not all of her own invention. One wonders what Willy thought of Claudine's clumsy attempt to bring Annie and Marcel together; Colette herself seems to have regretted it, for Claudine eventually admits that it was "worse than a blunder, it was a bad deed." Yet the inclusion of this episode is more than redeemed by the appeal of the book as a whole. During her early submissive period Colette may have tried to write fiction calculated to shock, and her reputation still suffers from the circumstances of her debut; but she never succeeded in producing Willy's type of sensationalism. There is nothing vicious about Annie,

3

for instance, and she has no sense of guilt. In making Annie relate stories from her past, Colette is mainly interested in their combined comedy and pathos; she also uses the contrast between Claudine and Annie to illustrate the contrast between two attitudes toward love, highlighting her own interest in the *ingénue libertine* figure, that "innocent libertine" Minne whose story she was soon to rewrite. At the same time, the femininity of her heroine's stepson, Marcel, reminds Claudine of Rézi, the woman she had loved a few years earlier. Claudine's love for Renaud might have formed a more satisfying contrast to Annie's type of attachment, which is purely physical, but unfortunately one cannot believe in it. Renaud is one of the least interesting of Colette's never very successful heroes, as she herself realized; but Claudine yearned for the ideal, and therefore her love had to be infinite.

There are other intriguing aspects to this book, the first full-length novel signed by the true author of the Claudine titles. The slightly arch *avertissement* or "notice" that prefaces it conceals a whole marital drama which was not resolved by the eventual divorce in 1910; in fact, perhaps Colette did not want to forget it. In the meantime she did not lose her sense of humor, for otherwise she would hardly have written the caricature of herself as "Willette Collie," the mime. Contemporary reviews and photographs indicate in fact that the caricature was not far from

4

the truth. It was also typical of Colette to waste no moment of her own experience; she had been on the stage barely a year when she began to use certain incidents in her writing, a foretaste of the many autobiographical themes which preoccupied her in the thirty or so books still to come.

In *Retreat from Love* the autobiographical elements were complex because they dealt not only with the present but with the past and the future. The "retreat," or more precisely "retirement," from the materialistic Parisian literary scene—Renaud was a writer, Léon Payet a novelist, and Maugis a music critic—documents the moment when Colette found her personal freedom. At the same moment she realized what mattered to her most; her memories, idealized like Claudine's love, of her village and her old house could live again as something more than memory through "Casamène," and she could live again too. Like Claudine, she could go for a walk in the snow, or observe the "filigree cups" of the wood anemones, or wonder whether it was more important to preserve the peaches or the dormice that ate them. The whole world was full of movement, light, color; the death of Renaud, the loss of love, need not mean death for her.

This is a novel of promise which was later to be entirely fulfilled. Colette develops here what the French poet Jules Supervielle was to call *oublieuse mémoire*, the memory that forgets because it selects, and, by its selection, creates. The erotic incidents in the book go back to the years with Willy and the popular taste of the early 1900s, but the emotional undertones and evocative descriptions take the reader forward to the next full-length novel, *La Vagabonde* (The Vagabond), serialized in *La Vie Parisienne* three years later, and to one of Colette's masterpieces of recollection, *La Maison de Claudine* (My Mother's House), of 1922.

Prologue

"Renaud, do you know what this is?"

He half-turned toward me, his newspaper on his knees; he had a cigarette in his left hand and held it some distance away, his little finger up in the air, just as a society lady holds a sandwich. . . .

"Oh, Renaud, keep that pose for a moment! It's the fashionable writer as his latest photograph would show him in *Fémina*. But guess what I've got here?"

He frowned as he peered at the little bit of rag that I was waving about, a little rag about an inch wide that had turned yellow.

"That? It's an old bandage that once wrapped up

7

a sore finger, I suppose. Throw it away, my dear; it looks dirty!"

I stopped laughing and went closer to my husband.

"It's not dirty, Renaud; it's just old. Look more closely. It's the shoulder piece from Rézi's nightdress . . ."

"Oh!"

He hadn't moved, but I knew him so well! His moustache, which was almost totally white, quivered imperceptibly, and his youthful eyes, as blue-black as pools of water, grew even blacker. How I love his display of emotion, and how proud I feel every time when I know that one single gesture on my part can stir the dark water of that gaze so deeply! I said it again:

"Yes, the shoulder piece from Rézi's nightdress . . . do you remember, Renaud?"

The ash from his cigarette fell on the carpet.

"Why have you kept it?" he asked without replying.

"I don't know. Are you cross?"

"Very. You know very well . . ."

He lowered his eyelids, as he always did when he was going to tell the truth.

"You know very well that I've tried with all my heart to blot out the memory that comes between us. I've tried to . . ."

"I haven't, Renaud, I haven't!"

8

He was about to be hurt—I reached out, with my voice and my arms:

"Understand me, darling, I'm not hiding anything from you; listen to why I've kept this bit of rag; see where I kept it and in what company!"

I sat down, placing the drawer on my knees.

"There's an old exercise book from school. There's an envelope where I collected the petals from a pale pink and white rose when I left Montigny. Here's the little purse in blue and yellow silk that Luce knitted for me. It's ugly and touching. There's a telegram from you . . . photographs from the theater at Bayreuth, a little dried-up lizard that I found on the ground, a shoe from my black mare, the one who had to be put down. Look, there are all the letters from Annie Samzun, and next to them photographs of Marcel in his flower costume. . . . There are little pink pebbles from the path at Les Vrimes, some of my hair when I had it long, rolled round into a coil. Look, that's you: that snapshot of you at Monte Carlo where you're so utterly ridiculous and so perfectly elegant! Why shouldn't I have kept the little piece of lawn that you describe as a bandage? It's there to remind me of one moment of our life *à deux,* one moment when we were both selfish and silly enough to think—not for long—that we could lead it *à trois.* . . . Let me keep it, Renaud; let it remain in the dateless tangle of our past! Short and delicious and quickly over, the bustling life of idle, busy people! I plunge into it without thinking of the future and I see my own reflection, for I can find nothing except ourselves! No, no, you're wrong, Rézi is *us* as well. It was a slightly more dangerous detour, a path where I almost lost you, where you let go of my hand, dear. . . . Oh, if you knew how much I thought about it! Call me without bitterness your armchair traveler! I remember passionately how I suffered at the time, just as one imagines, from the depths of a warm bed, the cold outside, the rain on the back of your neck, a pebbly road in the suburbs with trees groaning in the wind—don't take one scrap of our past away from me! Instead add some rings to this headdress which I keep like some wild, unsociable girl, where I hang flowers, iridescent shells, scraps of mirror glass, diamonds and amulets . . ."

"There wouldn't be any room for you, my darling child, in this echoing, highly polished hospital where every surface is gleaming white, frozen from reflecting the sky, nothing but the sky! Your eyes, my delightful little creature, would surely have lost their restless golden light, your eyes which seem always to reflect the shadow of a swaying branch. And besides, it's forbidden! Don't worry, read this without anxiety pulling at your beloved mouth and taking your short upper lip higher. In my room, hanging on the icy wall, there's a set of rules where all the brackets have the same shape as your upper lip: it's the only *objet d'art* which adorns the bareness of the place. My child, as I said, leave your old husband within the four walls of this refrigerator. It's the way to treat fish that have lost their freshness. . . .

"I can't sleep yet, Claudine. They don't know why. One very gentle doctor—so gentle that I think I've gone mad and they're afraid of upsetting me—assures me that this insomnia is quite normal. Very normal, definitely. My sleepy little bee, you who sleep silently with your forehead against your arms, do you hear what they say? It's very normal —especially at the beginning. Let's wait for the end.

"Apart from this unimportant detail, all's well. Words such as 'phenomena of nutrition,' 'digestive organs,' the 'larger intestine,' 'laziness of the heart' (laziness of the heart, Claudine!) beat against the smooth walls of my room like beautiful moths. . . .

"Write to me. Can you see how clear and upright my handwriting is? That's because I'm concentrating. All the best to Annie. And nothing for you except my poor tired arms, since I'm not allowed to have you . . ."

Renaud

"I've no news of Marcel. Keep an eye on him. He had some serious money worries last month."

I sat there, my back limp, my hands upturned, like a servant girl: a girl in the Puisaye engaged to be married who's just read a letter from her young man saying he's off to the wars—she couldn't have had eyes more forlorn or thoughts more numb than mine. . . . Renaud was there, and I was here. I was here, and Renaud was there. . . . This notion of there and here, Switzerland and Casamène, gave a wearisome impression of moving to and fro, the clicking of an empty shuttle. . . .

A timid little voice spoke behind me, "Is it good news?"

I turned away with a sigh: "Good news, yes, Annie, thank you."

Her head was bent over her embroidery frame, a kind of tambourine covered with flowered silk. Her smooth hair was absolutely black, black without any chestnut or blue, black of a kind that astonishes and satisfies the gaze. When you see Annie's hair by daylight you aren't tempted by any comparison, neither the blueness of the swallow nor the gleam of freshly broken-up anthracite, nor the wild black of the otter. . . . It's as black . . . as itself, and that's all there is to it. Her hair crowns her with a smooth, tightly fitting cap which is brought down slightly over one ear by parting at the side. A heavy pony tail, twisted in artless fashion, hangs down over the nape of her neck.

No creature is more gentle, more obstinate, more modest than Annie. She has kept no vanity, no bitterness or rancor from her three-year-long flight and her much-talked-about divorce. She lives at Casamène all year—all the year? Who knows? Not even I, her only friend. Her Kabylian-type skin doesn't age, and I find it hard to discover, in the fresh blue of her eyes, the secret security of knowing oneself better, of belonging completely to oneself. Through her bearing she remains the schoolgirl with the cowed shoulders. In the midst of this russet garden she seems a captive. She embroiders willingly, sitting by the window, idle and silent. Eugénie Grandet or Philomène de Watteville?

I'm a lazy vagabond who enjoys listening to others' travel adventures, but I haven't been able to extract anything from my embroideress with the long eyelashes. Sometimes she rouses herself and begins: "One day at Budapest, the same evening when I was insulted by that coachman . . ." "What coachman, Annie?" "A coachman . . . like—like any other coachman. Didn't I tell you about him?" "No. You were saying that one day, near Budapest—" "One day . . . oh! I only wanted to say that the hotels are so bad in that country! And the bedrooms are so uncomfortable, if only you knew!" At that she lowered her eyelashes, as though she had said something indecent.

Yet she had seen countries, skies, houses built from foreign granite, a deeper mauve or bluer than ours; she had seen arid countries, dried up by the sun, fields made spongy and thick with invisible water, cities which I'd describe, with my eyes shut, as belonging to the other side of the earth. . . . Have all those fleeting images not yet touched the depths of her eyes?

At the moment I'm living with Annie and I tolerate her presence without effort, because I love her with a kind of animal-like chaste friendship, and because I'm free when I'm with her, free to think, to be silent, to go away, to come back when I want to. I'm the one who says "I'm hungry," who rings for tea, who tames or teases the gray cat, and Toby dog follows me in fanatic fashion. In fact I'm the hostess: I become expansive in rocking chairs and I poke the fire, while Annie, half-sitting on a cane chair, embroiders as though she were a poor relation. Sometimes it makes me feel ashamed and irritated: really she's exaggerating her absentmindedness, her self-effacement: "Annie, the path's been blocked for three days where the wall's fallen down, you know." "Yes, I know." "Perhaps you ought to tell them to repair it?" "Yes, perhaps . . ." "You will?" "If you wish." I get angry.

"But my dear girl, I think *you* ought to do it!"

She raises her delightful eyes, her needle poised.

"Me? It's all the same to me."

"Oh really! It embarrasses me."

"Tell the gardener."

"But I don't give the orders here!"

"Oh yes you do, Claudine. Give them all; repair the walls, cut the wood, bring in the hay, I'll be so pleased! Give me the illusion that nothing belongs to

15

me, that I can get up from this chair and go, leaving nothing of me behind except this embroidery that I've started . . ."

Suddenly she fell silent and shook her head, while her pony tail flapped against her shoulders. And I have the wall repaired, the dead wood faggoted, the trees lopped and the aftermath brought in from the hayfields—these are things I know about!

I've been at Casamène for about a month—a month while Renaud has been freezing up there, high up on the Engadine. It's not grief that I'm enduring; something's lacking; it's like an amputation, a physical malaise so indefinable that I confuse it with hunger, thirst, migraine, or fatigue. It shows itself in brief attacks, idle yawning and spiteful dejection.

My poor darling! At first he didn't want to tell me anything: he concealed his Parisian neurasthenia and overwork. He had begun to believe in coca wines, pepto-iron, all pepsins, and one day he fainted while lying beside me. It was too late to talk about going into the country, taking things quietly, making a little tour. I immediately guessed the word that the uncommunicative doctors were keeping at the tips of their tongues, the word sanatorium. . . .

Renaud didn't want to go: "Look after me, Claudine! You'll cure me better than they will!" And in his dulled blue-black eyes I could read his jealous anger at leaving me alone in Paris, such proprietary panic that I burst out laughing and crying all at once —and I went to join Annie at Casamène, to please Renaud.

I stood up. I had to write to a coach builder, to the secretary of the *Revue Diplomatique*, to the furrier who stores my furs; I had to send the quarterly rent to Paris, what else? I felt tired in advance. Renaud used to deal with nearly everything. Oh, how slack and undevoted I am! I'll write to Renaud first, to give myself the strength.

"I'm going to write some letters, Annie. Aren't you going out?"

"No, Claudine, I'll still be here."

Her submissive eyes sought my approval; as I passed her I kissed the gleaming smooth hair which had never been curled or waved, the plainly dressed hair which smelled only like the fur of some clean animal. This shoulder which yields softly beneath my hand, it's not the one I'd like to clasp! When will that shoulder be restored to me, the one that's higher than me, the one I climb up as a cat might do, clinging to it with every finger? I only like kisses which come from above and I bend my head back to receive them, like an encounter with sweet summer rain. . . .

My young friend felt something in my kiss:

"Claudine—is Renaud really all right?"

I bit my tongue hard; I don't know any better cure for tears.

"Yes, really, my dear. His handwriting's firm, he's eating and resting. He's even asked me to keep an eye on Marcel. Marcel's too old for nursemaids, I think. I'm ready to send him money—just!"

"He's very young, isn't he?"

I protested. "Very young!—not so young as all that! We're the same age, Marcel and I."

"That's what I meant," insinuated Annie, who has good manners.

I smiled to her in the glass over the chimneypiece. Very young . . . no, I'm no longer very young. I've kept my figure, my freedom of movement; I still have my tight covering of flesh which fits me without a crease . . . but I've changed all the same. I know myself so well! My chestnut-colored hair, which is thick and dressed in coils, still offsets my slightly over-pointed chin which everyone finds "witty." My mouth has lost its gaiety, and beneath my eyes, their orbits more voluptuous but also more hollow, is the long stretch of my cheek, less velvety, less rounded; the daylight, as it falls on my face, already shows up the line—is it a dimple still, or already a wrinkle?—patiently carved there by my smile. . . . Other people don't know all this. I'm the only one to notice the first disintegration. I'm in no way bitter about it. One day a woman will see me and say: "Claudine's tired today." A few months later one of Renaud's friends will meet me: "I saw Claudine today; she's caught a real case of old age this summer!" And then—and then . . .

What difference does it make if Renaud doesn't want to learn that I'm growing old? The essential thing at the moment is never to leave him anymore, not to let him forget me for twenty-four hours so that he hasn't time to think about me, for he re-creates me every moment in the guise of a fresh young girl whose horizontal eyes, "bracketlike" upper lip, and bronze hair turned him into a young man in love once again.

When he comes back, I'll be wearing my warpaint: a touch of blue kohl between my eyelashes, on my cheeks a dusting of powder, the same shade of ecru as my skin; I'll have brushed my teeth to enliven my mouth . . . good heavens, what am I thinking of? Surely I must forget my entrance on stage, I must hurry to support him, he'll be tired after his journey, I must carry him away and fill him with myself, occupy all the air he breathes?

I looked away from the glass where Annie's eyes encountered my thoughts. . . .

Autumn here is dazzling. Annie lives among this blaze of color cold and unmoved, almost indifferent, and she makes me angry. Casamène is perched on the rounded shoulder of a little hill roughened with stunted oaks which have not yet been licked by the flames of October. Roundabout, this countryside, which I already love, includes the harshness of the south with the mistral blowing, the blue pines of the east, and from the gravel path up on the terrace you can see, far away in the distance, the gleam of a cold river, silver and rapid-flowing, the color of a minnow.

The boundary wall collapses onto the road, the

Virginia creeper stealthily saps the strength from the wistarias, and the rose trees which no one looks after produce double flowers and grow wild again. All that remains of the maze that was naïvely planned by Annie's grandfather is a tangle of maples, service trees, and thickets of what the Montigny people call "pulains," clumps of old-fashioned Weigela. The fir trees are a hundred years old and won't see another century, for the ivy's growing tightly round their trunks and stifling them. What sacrilegious hand moved the sundial's slate face on its stand, it shows noon at a quarter to two?

The old apple trees produce tiny fruit that you might use for trimming hats, but a stem from a muscat grapevine, nourished by some secret source, has shot up vigorously, covered a hen house and pulled it down, then, grasping the arm of a cherry tree, has smothered it in leaves, tendrils, and plum-dark grapes that are already falling one by one. There's a disturbing luxuriance here flanking the bare poverty-stricken mauve rocks that pierce the ground, where even the brambles can find nothing on which to hang their barbed-wire leaves.

Annie's house is an old, low, single-story house, warm in the winter and cool in summer, a place without adornment but not without grace. The little carved marble pediment—discovered by a well-read grandfather—is flaking and moldering away, quite yellow, and under the five loose stone steps a toad sings amorously, his throat full of pearls. At dusk he drives away the last midges, the little grubs which live in the cracked stones. From time to time he looks at me deferentially, but with reassurance, then— leaning one hand against the wall in human fashion he stands up to swallow—I hear the *nop* sound of his wide mouth. When he rests he moves his eyelids in such a pensive and lofty way that I haven't yet dared say a word to him. Annie is too scared of him to do him any harm.

A little later comes a hedgehog, a muddle-headed, scatter-brained creature, bold yet easily frightened, who scuttles along in a nearsighted way, goes into the wrong hole, eats greedily, is frightened of the car and makes a noise like a young pig on the loose. The gray cat hates him, but hardly ever goes near him, and her green eyes grow bitter when she looks at him.

A little later still, a very small delicate bat brushes against my hair. It's the moment when Annie shivers, goes in and lights the lamp. I stay a little longer to watch the broken arcs described by the bat which screeches as it flies, with a sound like a fingernail on a window pane. And then I go back in to the drawing room, pink with light, where Annie is embroidering close to the lamp.

"Annie, how I love Casamène!"

"Do you really? That's good!"

She was sincere and affectionate, quite brown in the pink light.

"Just imagine, I love it as though it were something of mine!"

The blue of her eyes grew slightly darker: it's her way of blushing. . . .

"Annie, don't you think that Casamène is one of the fascinating and melancholy ends of the world, a place just as much in the past, just as far from the present as that daguerreotype of your grandfather?"

She hesitated. "Yes, I liked it once, when I was little. I believed in the maze, in the endlessness of the pathway that turns back onto itself . . . I've been put off Casamène. I just rest there . . . I put myself there . . . there or somewhere else . . ."

"I don't believe it!" I said, shaking my head. "It's a place I wouldn't give to anyone; if Casamène were mine—"

"It is," she said softly.

"Yes, it is, and you go with it . . . but—"

"Casamène is yours," insisted Annie with her gentle obstinacy. "I'm giving it to you."

"Come on now, you're crazy!"

"No, no, I'm not as crazy as that! You'll see, when I leave again, I'll give you Casamène . . ."

I sat up with a start and looked her in the face. She had just cut off a needleful of silk and put her scissors down beside her. Leave again! She looked as though she were going to sit there forever!

"Are you being serious, Annie?"

"In giving you Casamène? Of course I'm serious."

"No, I mean . . . are you thinking of leaving again?"

She made me wait for a moment, giving a sidelong glance toward the gleaming window and the heavy darkness that pressed against it. She raised a finger.

"Hush! Not tonight, in any case . . ."

Her enigmatic expression immediately intrigued me. It's so enjoyable to see people suddenly emerge and reveal themselves—through pride, thoughtlessness, or simply through a mischievous urge to surprise—to reveal themselves clearly and say: "I'm not the person you thought I was!" There's pleasure in growing fond of the people who deceive us, who wear falsehood like a highly elaborate dress and only remove it through a voluptuous desire for nudity. I didn't love Renaud any less when he was deceiving me, and who knows if the image of Rézi hasn't remained dearer to me for what she concealed than for what she granted?

The passive Annie, who makes people shrug their shoulders out of kindly pity, who would have believed it of her? She shook off her husband and her marriage, simply, without any fuss, like those lithe dogs that you put on a leash, then they slip out of their collars with nothing worse than a scrape to their ears.

"So you want to go away again, Annie? Do you?"

She sucked a finger she had pricked and shook her head like a child.

"I didn't say anything of the kind—let's be fair! I'm going on a short trip . . ."

How I enjoyed her studied air; she looked like the perfect notary, her lips sealed by professional etiquette.

"Good heavens, Annie, you don't need to be so formal with me! If you want to go, then go! In any case don't let *my* presence hold you back!"

"Don't get upset, Claudine! There's no question of going . . . not yet. Only—"

"Only?"

She brought her chair closer, placed her hands on my lap and let them nestle there as though she were laying down her heart, her heart overflowing with the need to speak, or to be silent. She looked toward the windows again, as though afraid that the weight of soft darkness leaning against them might shatter them into pieces.

The moment was just as mysterious as midnight. No sound came from the distant kitchen, but rats could be heard clawing their way along between the floorboards . . . the wind, already strong, occasionally blew puffs of pine-scented smoke from the charred logs back down the chimney, and the gray cat announced the approaching cold by tucking all her paws beneath her. The lamplight shone brightly over Annie's skirt up to her knees; but her face, long and slim as a hazelnut, remained in a dark rosy glow like a statuette of pink clay. She took hold of my hands; she was very close to me; she opened and closed her mouth. She was going to speak . . . no . . . yes. . . .

"Listen, Claudine . . ."

"I'm listening, my dear."

"You don't know what it feels like, do you, wanting to go away?"

"Well . . . there's much to be said on that subject, and it might be a mistake to imagine that I don't sometimes think of . . . going off on a little trip . . ."

"Don't laugh! I want you to understand me. Wanting to go away . . . lots of people don't suspect what it is. It's an illness, a form of poisoning; it's not even an idea, Claudine! I swear to you it's not really a mental thing. I'd rather compare it to . . . to a cyst that you carry about with you, something that grows slowly; you feel it getting bigger every day. While I'm eating, while I'm asleep or doing embroidery, it's here, there, all around me, the thing that tugs at me persistently: wanting to go away. You wouldn't realize it, would you? Or am I bad at hiding it?"

With her hands and shoulders she made pathetic gestures like an invalid seeing a doctor; she tried to locate her pain, she felt her head and her sides; her eyes, which are mauve in the evening, questioned me . . . I stroked her hair to soothe her. . . .

"Poor pet! You should have told me . . . What country tempts you so strongly?"

She shrugged her shoulders wearily:

"How do I know? It's all the same to me, provided that . . ."

"Oh, well, then . . . you need a ticket for the suburban railway."

She didn't laugh, and went on:

"You must realize, Claudine, I'm not saying I *will* go away. I *want* to go away!"

"And you're restraining yourself. That's how people ruin their health."

"Oh, my health . . . I've known worse!"

A strange, ambiguous irony had just entered her eyes. I drew back a little, as though my friend Annie were suddenly disguised in front of me as a little prostitute.

"I mightn't know, Annie. You used to tell me everything once."

I was lying, for Annie had never talked much about herself. But the reproach touched her.

"I'd like to tell you everything, Claudine . . . but there's far, far too much!"

At each "far" she bent her head lower, shaking it like someone turning a vase upside down and shaking it empty in two movements.

"You can just tell the worst things . . ."

The same lingering, lascivious gaze as she turned away . . . then she slid down to my feet in a childish need for physical humility, a feminine instinct for kneeling in devotion.

"I've done everything, Claudine, everything! and I've never told anyone about it!"

Then she buried her head in my hands and waited . . . for what? For me to scold her? To make her tell her beads thirty times over? To forgive her? I teased her:

"Everything? That's not much, you know! I've often thought sadly how monotonous the business of love-making is."

She raised her head with its tousled hair, her expression shocked and amazed, and her eyes seemed to have grown blue again in the darkness of my lap.

"Monotonous . . . well, you're hard to please, really!"

I burst out laughing, the admission was so frank, so admiring, full of wholehearted, utterly new respect for the business of love-making.

"Congratulations, Annie! Congratulations . . . especially to him!"

She stood up, modestly tightened the buckle of her belt and pinned into place a lock of black hair which hung down over her contrite cheek.

"There's no *him*, Claudine."

"Oh, should I have said *her*?"

The remains of a strange little snake, which I had thought dead, writhed within me.

"No, not that either!" admitted Annie, in a low voice. "It's—*them* . . ."

"*Them!* Oh, well . . ."

I was bewildered and could say no more. How many? Seven, or three hundred? A couple or a battalion? Them! I felt a kind of deference, the respect inspired by the impossible, I whose untamed body could only give itself to one man. . . .

A sigh responded to mine . . . a sigh from the prostrate dog Toby, one of those deep, ridiculous bull-terrier sighs which seemed torn from his emotional breast by the tragedy of the universe. Toby has tact and a sense of situation. Annie, whose eyes were moist, laughed nervously, and Toby raised toward us the white eyeballs of a devoted slave. . . . Our relaxation ended in helpless laughter, and Annie fell into my arms.

"I'll tell you everything, Claudine! All I know, at least."

"What do you mean? All you 'know'! Was it a case of sleepwalking?"

"No. . . . Let me go on with my embroidery to give myself countenance."

Lying back comfortably in a chair as deep as a hip bath, I awaited the splendid story. In front of me Annie's head, with its swallowlike coiffure, stood out against the cretonne cover, which possessed the comforting honesty of glaring bad taste. My friend spent too long collecting her thoughts: I was afraid she would lose heart, and I began:

"Once upon a time—"

"Once upon a time," she repeated in docile fashion, "there was a hotel in Baden, beside a little river where spitting was forbidden, surrounded by lawns which were swept with a broom every morning. It was terribly hot, there was music everywhere, electric light in every corner, bedrooms that were too white and too cheerful, and I wasn't cheerful enough. There was a dining room glittering with endless tables, all the women wore diamonds and the men were dressed like Toby, in black, with dazzling white fronts. Oh, I was dark in body and soul among all that glitter! I should tell you that at the little table next to mine I had a neighbor . . ."

"Ah ha!"

"He'd picked up my sunshade for me. No, it hadn't started like that! I'd met him on the stairs, and he'd said to me . . . No, he hadn't spoken to me that time; but there's a way of looking, isn't there? And at table, too. . . . Oh, Claudine, I don't know what I'm saying now! I'll never be able to tell everything. When I tell it briefly it sounds so crude . . ."

Her needleful of silken thread became tangled, her skin grew clammy, and she was upset.

"But it doesn't matter, my dear! Go on, go on, just the main facts."

She rested breathlessly for a moment, her eyelids flickered, and, lowering her voice, she went on.

"Well, this is what happened. One evening he came into my room and I didn't know his name. Just imagine! He was handsome, dark like me, with such an imperious manner that I thought of Alain and felt weak, as though I was going to collapse. I thought that everything was starting all over again, that fate was punishing me for having left; that another yoke, worse than the first one, was going to enslave me once again. . . ."

"And then?"

"And then, good heavens, how can I tell you?— at the mere touch of his bare hands I no longer knew who I was, and as for him, I didn't mind at all that I didn't know his name! He spoke to me, using horrible words . . ."

She looked away and I saw the muscles in her neck swelling.

"He taught me . . . disgusting things, things that nobody does . . . or, at least, I thought so. . . . He treated me like . . ."

"Like a tart . . ."

"That's it! And I tolerated everything without complaining. I felt that I was lying in water, that I was just a body whose pores possessed five senses for enjoying sin. Think . . . just think, I barely looked at him! I looked at him once and for all, and I saw immediately that he was handsome without looking noble, I saw the whiteness of his teeth and his eyeballs, the dark outlines of his muscles, his gleaming hair, which was too curly; and then I closed my eyes, so that I'd feel better. For a moment, I remember, I felt giddy as though I were on a swing. I opened my eyes again. I was lying across the bed, almost sliding off it, my head thrown back, and I could only see the base of an armchair, the pattern on the carpet, the end of my plaited hair that was hanging down . . . God knows what he could have been doing to me at that moment!"

"Weren't you curious enough to find out?"

She removed her hands from her guilty face, and her eyes, blue and empty, their pupils no more than specks of black ink, contemplated through mine the burning memory.

"Seeing is much less important," she murmured in a tired voice.

"I don't agree with you, Annie."

And my memories of the past, of yesterday, led me to bite, on my lips, the shape of other lips. . . .

"But what about the next day, Annie?"

"Ah, Claudine, that was the worst of all! Naturally, in the morning, when I was all alone, I didn't even dare to look at myself in the glass. I was dying of hunger and I didn't ring the bell. I told myself: You wretched creature, can you still think about eating, about living like everyone else! You're going to go downstairs, meet that . . . that creature, sit down in the same dining room with him, perhaps he's going to say good morning to you, and you don't even know his name . . ."

"I'd have gone straight to the hotel reception desk to ask for it."

"That's what I did," she said naïvely.

"I'm sure he had a fine composite Spanish name, didn't he, with *y*'s to separate each part?"

"Not a bit of it!" she cried, almost angrily. "He was called Martin."

"Not even Martinez? He could have done that for you, now really!"

She bent her head, but not quickly enough to prevent me from seeing her strange smile, one that belonged to an Annie I didn't know.

"He'd done so many things for me," she insinuated with gentle remoteness.

"And then, Annie, the next night?"

"The next night?"

She looked at me with wide open limpid eyes, and said proudly:

"The next night I packed my trunks and left for Nuremberg."

"Oh, how silly! Why?"

"I was frightened," whispered Annie, looking down. "Frightened of starting again, frightened of becoming the regular prey of that man, frightened of losing my freedom, yes, my freedom, that was still quite new and gauche! . . . and then, you know, Claudine, I think it was that young man who took my pink pearl . . ."

What could I say? Poor Annie . . . the incident was commonplace, and if it had lasted more than one night it would have become sordid.

Annie was silent; what could she see in her mind's eye? The pattern of the carpet, the base of the armchair, the end of a plait of black hair hanging down as she lay with her head thrown back.

"Annie! Annie!"

"What?" she said with a start.

"Go on! . . . chapter two . . . the second divine passer-by . . ."

"I'm thirsty," she said.

"Yes, you'll have something to drink. But go on first. I'm not going to ring now and call in Augusta to see you looking hot, with your hair all undone. I don't know what she'd think."

She yielded to my request, as to the desire for the unknown.

"There was no sequel right away, Claudine. I ran away from that man as I had run away from Alain; I took fright fairly quickly at that time, and for the first few days I thought I was free of him and also from myself. Ah, Claudine, that's really where the trouble starts. The wanting, Claudine, the wanting of the most physical, the most urgent, the most credulous and desperate kind. Yes, credulous, don't you understand? You must realize that I behaved like some stupid schoolgirl, in the exclusive power of that unknown man I was running away from! I believed, and I cried over it, that some sovereign chance had cast me, naked and submissive, across the path of that man, the man made of the same flesh as myself, my male 'double,' the man of whom I seemed to be the hollow and exact reproduction.

"The day when I received a reply by telegram from the hotel in Baden—for I'd written: 'Monsieur Martin left for unknown destination,' Claudine, that day I began to cry aloud, holding out my arms toward everything he was taking away from me! I wanted to die, to send agents to look for him; I wanted to drink ether . . . until . . ."

"Until, darling?"

She laid her head on my shoulder with a happy sigh of satisfaction.

"Until I realized that another man, several other men, many other men could give me what my near-ignorance was yearning for . . ."

What a periphrasis! I moved Annie's head away from me so that I could see her better. She had the lowered eyelids and the smile of some virgin who had drifted into sleep and died while contemplating the faces of angels. But she spoke, and the fervor of her gratitude—"My thanks to all of them!"—was expressed in such touching fashion that I felt somewhat disturbed.

"As from that day, Claudine, I knew what life was!—a garden where you can pick everything, eat everything, leave everything and come back for it again. Changing isn't infidelity, because in fact I only love and I only satisfy myself. Ah, Claudine! How the scales fell from my eyes and how confidently I've looked at men, all men, since that boy who was the second one—"

"What boy?"

"One of the hotel pages at Carlsbad. Do you know Carlsbad? There are still Jews there, dressed like Jews, with surcoats stiff with dirt, beautiful Christ-like hair, and little chamber pots on their heads. Some Austrians spit as they walk past them—"

"Yes—and the page?"

"He was delightful!" said Annie in an unconsciously casual way. "They pick them specially, you know. A little blond Viennese, very conscientious—a typically good servant."

This was the unknown speaking now, straightforward and unashamed, with the upturned smiling lips of a connoisseur. The delectable warmth of discoveries brought a glow to my cheeks.

"A typically good servant, I tell you! He was always afraid he wasn't doing enough or wasn't doing it well enough. He brought up my mail morning and evening; I remember his little pink face the evening when he respectfully informed me, holding his braided cap, that for two days his friend Hans would be replacing him on that floor."

She laughed as she lay back against my knees; she

laughed with nervous little sighs, like someone cough-
ing. Oh dear, she laughed too much! We were going
to have a tiresome *crise de nerfs*. No, thank goodness,
dinner was announced!

$\mathcal{A}$nnie's confession, or should I say, explosion, has left me shattered. I'd asked to see "the landscapes of her mind"—she showed me landscapes all right, as Maugis would say, to a disturbing extent! And, unknown to me, the affection I felt for her must have changed: Annie led me to feel more respect for her but less concern. She'd liberated herself, yes, body and soul, but I'm slightly cross with her for having told me her secret so quickly. Or rather, I'd have preferred another sort of secret; I wanted it to be unique, different from that of so many women, more of an exception. How guilty her husband was! No one realizes just what risks a woman's taking when the first man she sleeps with is a fool. A little demi-semi junior god, promoted to the lowly tasks of love, preserved Annie from what old Mélie used to call "bad illnesses;" he deserves to be thanked for it. My friend's bravado was equal to her unawareness of the danger: Brieux hadn't yet made any impression on simple souls. . . .

A letter from my dearly beloved assured me that he was well:

> . . . A long open, sunny balcony, day beds, your old husband lying in one of them, wrapped up in blankets, an atmosphere of mineral-like brilliance, its resonance painful at first and then attractive . . . a naked, deceptive sun, chilly and golden like mountain wine. . . .

How sad to know that he's like other invalids! And why am I so proud that I only want *special* people in my affections? Everything that identifies them with the rest of the world makes me angry with them and with myself. And then I find it so difficult to write freely to Renaud! I'm only good at loving him, alas! I've lived too long with him, beside him, in him; my letters turn out clumsy, cold, or else they prevaricate like a sulky schoolgirl who doesn't want to play her *valse-caprice*. Can he recognize me through them, at least? Does he guess that I'm tense, scowling and bad-tempered, just as I am when I love him most? His absence and my stay at Casamène make my past life recede and I take stock of myself. I'm alone in spite of Annie, very much alone. . . .

Are there many women in the world as solitary as I am, in spite of Renaud, because of him? Or is it the very simple, common fate of women who have given their whole selves, once and for all?

No women friends around me—Annie is only an affectionate attendant. One single memory, bitter-sweet, the image of a prickly flower streaked with black and pink which made our fingers bleed: Rézi. Renaud and I no longer mention her. We've kept fear, shame, suffered jealousy, and vanity as well, because we made each other suffer, the secret satisfaction of having dealt and returned a well-aimed blow. What does the rest matter? Wouldn't I forget in the space of an hour all those who call themselves my friends? In Renaud's absence there's only one heart where I can take refuge and find myself more solitary still: the heart from where grow the deep tree roots, the grass with its thousand swords—from where emerge, young and vital, the insects with their antennae still folded, the grass snakes, striped and moving like a furtive stream—from where come the spring, the wheat, and the wild rose. . . .

When my reason for living, by name Renaud, is no longer there, shall I find within myself—that self on whom solitude once acted like a slightly heady and dangerous tonic—shall I find within myself, when alone, that bitter and rejuvenating consolation which has kept my heart intact, even if darkened and beating more slowly?

I was born solitary, I grew up without mother, brother or sister, with a restless father whom I could have taken under my wing, and I've lived without women friends. Hasn't such emotional isolation created within me a spirit which is just cheerful enough, just sad enough, which flares up at little and flickers out for no reason at all, not kind, not destructive, unsociable in fact and closer to animals than to mankind? Courage I have, physical courage—a fine merit when one is frightened of nothing—a fine confidence in my nerves which obey me, dutifully, controlled by my senses. Honesty . . . perhaps, but dressed like a tart. Pity, hardly for the miserable species to which I belong, because it often chooses to be wretched, and, in addition, I have the ability to be kind when I'm in love . . . ? "In love," feeble words to express so much! Imbued, that's a better way of putting it—imbued, that's it, imbued in body and soul, for unchanging love entered so deeply into the whole of my being that I almost expected to see my hair and skin change color.

The animals here are delightful. There's the dog Toby, an old friend, and Péronnelle, a totally new autocrat. I've known Toby for a long time, and his understanding of our race tells him pretty clearly that I'm his real mistress: he considers Annie as a subordinate. At the age of five he's preserved his childlike soul to which all is pure, even falsehood. He's a bull terrier with a weak heart, a heart that's always at the point of giving out but never does. He sighs mysteriously like his brother the toad, that other snubnosed, brindled creature with beautiful eyes, and although he runs after vagrants with dust-clad feet, puffing and foaming at the

43

mouth, he thinks it sensible to give a wide berth to a devout and well-armed praying mantis when he sees her saying her prayers in the middle of a path.

Péronnelle has none of these childish fears. This hospital patient, who was dying of hunger in the grass where Annie found her, has a modest gray coat, but its fabric is the silkiest imaginable velvet, which melts in your hand and turns silver in the sunshine. Nothing flashy, none of those parrotlike stripes. Two black collars around her neck, three bracelets around her front paws, a muscular tail and a distinguished chin, with regal green eyes which look straight at you—insolent, tender eyes with upturned corners and accentuated with kohl. Péronnelle, when she's angry, wouldn't yield to God the Father, let alone me. She purrs, licks her lip, bites, and taps, while the whole house is kept in step.

"Péronnelle," said Annie the other day, "reminds me of my sister-in-law Marthe, but she's more likable."

Péronnelle, who's as restless as a dog, fills Casamène with dovelike cooing and flutelike cries. When the lamps are lit she's exultant; she tears up the newspapers, steals balls of thread, puts on invisible sabots and gallops about like a foal, jumping onto the middle of the table, where she turns into a friendly little battering ram pushing against our chins with her strong forehead; she scrapes Annie's cheek with a tongue like a toothbrush and uses my head as a gangway from where she jumps onto the chimneypiece.

She loves me already, although I don't forget my dear Fanchette from the past. . . . Poor white Fanchette, who had such a delightful character; she was a modern provincial and applied herself so conscientiously to everything in life! She slept very soundly, ran about a lot, ate at great length, and hunted assiduously. What happened?—a chicken bone slightly sharper than usual . . . and the green gold of her eyes grew bloodshot, she clawed the air and her white pigeonlike throat—and there was no more Fanchette! So now I've left behind me my father, Fanchette and Mélie—I've outstripped them, I'm going a little further, not much further. . . .

Mélie left me, she grew suddenly old, as full of troubles as Saint Litvinne, twisted with rheumatism, her body swollen out with water; she was deaf and blind, I don't know what else, so much so that when we heard she was dead, we could only cry "At last!"

My splendid father, my father with his tricolor beard, he lost his life amongst his books, just like that! . . . His nose was pointing forward, perhaps from absentmindedness, he would so easily forget to have lunch or tie his tie. I understood slowly that he was dead, after a few days, when the echo of his fine aggressive voice no longer rang out between the walls of the house where I would look for him from room to room, like those obstinate dogs who know their master's out and yet push all the doors open with their noses: "He's not there. In the next room? No. Let's try the first one again, perhaps he went back while I was examining this one. . . ."

Renaud's letters continue to come, and the days are growing shorter. My dear husband is giving way to that touching weakness of well-cared-for invalids who show a belated interest in the working of their intestines, find they have a liver and a stomach, and become enthusiastic about definitions which explain nothing. Technical words slip into his letters; he uses them now without irony, with a touch of that pompous superiority affected by medical students. The regular routine of being weighed is becoming the anxious moment of his day, and the name of a certain Coucheroux, a neurasthenic and the rare case of the sanatorium, crops up three times in four pages. I'm not unkind, no . . . but if the said

Coucheroux and I could have a quarter of an hour together, he'd experience a new treatment for acute neurasthenia!

A letter from Marcel, a ridiculous one. He's trying it on, so hard that I'm not even angry. Three thousand francs! This child is ill. Have I got three thousand francs for that boy with the face of a tired girl? A nice hundred-franc note and half a dozen ironically pleasant lines: then my stepmother's conscience will be at ease.

Annie has fallen silent again and seems to be slightly embarrassed after her hysteria of the other evening. She walks about without a sound, prowling around me, with the contrite grace of a cat who has broken a vase.

This morning, shivering from sleepiness, she was standing on the broken steps which wobble underfoot like the unsteady stones indicating a ford across a stream. Seven o'clock was striking, and I was emerging from the maze, soaking wet from the dew, my nose dissolving and my hands numb, with a basket over my arm. The October morning had an intoxicating smell of fog, wood smoke, and rotting leaves. I had found a rougher kind of Fresnoy, more bony,

49

with rocks piercing through the grass, more russet with sunshine and frost. The wild perfume of that rust-colored dawn had got me out of my bed as far as the nest of torpid wasps that I'd had my eye on.

"Want a hazelnut, Annie?"

Annie's hand emerged from the pale blue dressing gown, which was the same color as her eyes. Her plait hung down to her waist, and the cold made her look more than ever like a poor little sick Arab. I pushed her hand away.

"You silly, see what it is, at least!"

For a moment she looked down uncomprehendingly at my basketful of the rough-ground mixture, yellow and black, gleaming with mother-of-pearl, moving feebly . . . I had scooped them up in spadefuls, this mash of torpid wasps, and I was hurrying to burn them in the stove, for their waxy smell sickened me. Annie contemplated them in quiet fright, her hands behind her back.

"What are you doing up at this hour, my dear?"

She looked up, her eyelids, fringed with their heavy lashes, swollen with sleep, or perhaps with sleeplessness.

"It's a telegram; they took it up to your bedroom, Claudine, and you'd already gone out. So I was looking for you—"

"A telegram?"

Renaud? Some accident? What was it? Oh, that wretched blue paper that sticks together! I stood there bent over the unpunctuated lines like Annie over the basketful of wasps.

She began to shiver with anxiety and cold.

"Well, Claudine?"

I held out the telegram to her. I was stupefied:

MAY I COME I'M GOING OUT OF MY MIND MARCEL

I was so relieved that I burst into indignant laughter.

"That's a fast one! Now what do you say to that? Oh, if only his father were there! Just wait! I'm going to send him back a little wire that he won't exactly enjoy!"

Annie, through prudence or indifference, said nothing, and with the tip of a hazel twig I angrily stirred up my heap of dead wasps.

"What are you going to do, Claudine?" she eventually found the courage to ask.

"Tell Renaud, of course! Or—"

No, I can't tell Renaud, crack the delicate shell of his rest, with the risk of a possible relapse; slow down his recovery; put off, even by one hour, the day when I'll be overcome all at once by my weakness; the day when he'll take me in his arms, arms that have grown young again. . . .

"Annie, tell me, what do *you* think I should do?"

She pursed her lips in a practical, vaguely prophetic way.

"My dear, let the child come. We'll see . . ."

I'm still angry. Marcel here! I can stand him in Paris, I tolerate his vice and show no resentment over his niggling feminine spitefulness. Basically he hardly changes: he merely goes through phases—dare I say phases of the moon?—which transform him, making him euphoric or depressed, after which he becomes himself again. For both Renaud and me Marcel remains the eighteen-year-old boy with bad habits—and yet, if I can count accurately, we were both twenty-seven in the same year! He leads the monotonous existence of cranks, bureaucrats, and little tarts—especially tarts. He yawns frequently, in a feeble, exhausted way, his arms outstretched, his back arched, and cries: "Good heavens I'm so bored! I've got nobody tonight!" He usually says that such and such a music-hall promenade is "good value," that "there aren't any smart Englishmen about this season," that "So-and-so, such a nice boy, has got mixed up with swindlers." He talks to me for hours about the reprehensible methods of the beauty institute where everything costs two louis, my dear, and where the creams ruin the skin. He talks about quince water, sterilized lanolin, goes crazy about Sofia water, benzoin solution and rose water; he drinks curdled milk and massages the lower part of his eyelids. He pesters Calliope van Langendonck with questions and asks this Ionian beauty about what is "good for the skin"—and then suddenly he disappears for three weeks, comes back looking drained, as pale and pink as a convolvulus flower. He's feverish, doesn't say a word, hardly answers you. He then confides in me briefly, calls a spade a spade and admits honestly in our fine language: "A gem, Claudine! A mind like a little schoolgirl. . . . He's at the Château d'Eau barracks . . ."

Renaud, who belongs to a less indulgent and less outspoken age, can't get used to his son. He's wrong. Sometimes Marcel profits from pity because he's "ill"; sometimes he flees from my husband's anger. Renaud talks of hitting him, sending him to the colonies, and so on. "The child," as I call him, tolerates the storms in silence, with a nasty look. I intervene kind-heartedly between father and son, for the sake of silence and calm rather than in the hope of improving matters, and my strange stepson seems grateful to me sometimes. It's for me that he reserves his most wheedling appeals: "Claudine, my pockets are empty, you know . . ." When I'm tired of telling him "It's because they've got holes in them," I hand over the louis and he makes off with it, kissing my hand with a sigh of relief: "What a good sort you are, Claudine. If you weren't a woman . . ."

Yes, all this happens in Paris. But to keep him here, if only for a week, this dubious little trinket, to hear his forced laugh, to feel his boredom between Annie and me . . . oh, no, no, no! I'll go as far as fifty louis, there! And then he can go away without disturbing my warm and bitter solitude, my secluded corner of russet earth smelling of boxwood, crowned with Virginia creeper, rounded like a gem amid the soft blue haze of the mountains: "My" Casamène! Annie's rash words: "I'm giving you Casamène!" reach right down to the center of my earthbound soul. Could this small island with its maze, its little marble pediment, its clumps of Judas trees and bladder nuts, this jewel, as old-fashioned as a brooch with a miniature, be mine? Later, with Renaud by my side, I could develop the Puisaye farmer instinct which came to me from ancestors who tended the soil and were jealous of their property. . . .

Already, when I'm exhausted through thinking of Renaud, counting the days, imagining his cheeks less hollow and his moustache whiter (he writes me this in childish despair), remembering his hands, the left one open, idle and generous, while the right closes over an absent fountain pen, when my brows become pained from too much thinking, then I turn toward Casamène, my new plaything. When I pick up a vine shoot I'm no longer indifferent about it . . . I fasten up the trailing vine with a twisted reed and tie up the rose trees, taking care of the "eyes" for next year. I dig the damp earth, the grass which is now withering, with thoughts worthy of the first man who won his land: "This clump of grass is mine; mine too is the rich soil below, the earthworm's hidden dwelling, the mole's winding corridor; mine too, deeper still, the rock that has never seen the light of day; mine too, if I wish, the dark and captive water buried a hundred feet down, and I, if I wish, will drink the first mouthful, tasting of sandstone and rust . . . !"

But—what about Montigny? This does not mean that Montigny is dwindling within my heart. My house at Montigny remains for me what it always was: a treasure, a lair, a citadel, the museum of my youth. . . . Why can't I encircle it, together with its garden as green as the sides of a well, with a wall which will hide it from all eyes! My decorous love suspends over it a mirage which deceives me alone! In this way Maître Frenhofer hatched his shapeless work away from the penetrating, mediocre gaze of men. Annie, and Marthe Payet, and Calliope van Langendonck, and the plump Maugis, if I showed them my house in Montigny, they'd say: "Well, it's only an old house."

It's not only an old house, you poor creatures! It's the house at Montigny. And when I die, it will die, too . . . When my eyes are ready to close forever, they will look up at its mauve slate roof embroidered with yellow lichen; at this sign the green of its flowerless garden will dissolve into a mist, the seven colors of a trembling prism will outline the bare bones of its dark hulk, and we will remain, the house and I, for one supreme second, half in this world, half in the next.

"Oh, my armchair traveler! . . ."

Poor, poor loved one, how clearly I hear his voice! I'm a little ashamed and sad. Don't I owe him all my thoughts? But they belong to him, since they come from me, and I depend on him like the sucker from a rosebush that runs under the ground, far from the main stem, before sending up to the light its first shoot, tender and gleaming, the color of a brownish pink earthworm. . . .

Today, unseasonal August sunshine is scorching us, making us feel dazed and strange. Yesterday morning there was a frost. Annie says nothing; she's sitting on the ground beside me, leaning against a cherry tree that dates from last century, its trunk broad enough to support the two of us. Her eyes are closed and she turns her face passively toward the light, motionless in a way that no longer deceives me. It was like this, surely, that she held up her face to be kissed by those whom she worships like so many gods—men!

She's looking inward, indifferent to this day borrowed from summer, this unique day when I savor each hour, when I press each blue shadow into the herbal of my memory. Ah, Renaud, is it possible that the air surrounding you gleams with ice and the little bright beads on your long moustache sparkle when you breathe? I see this and it hurts me: it takes me too far away from you!

In the near-burning air the leaves from the weeping acacia—an old stunted creature with a short trunk and branches like twisted arms—fall one by one, in a gentle rain, barely spinning before they settle. The autumn has drained them of color down to the white of their green ivory.

The cooing of a turtle dove, rapid and guttural, comes closer to us. Péronnelle has found us and is coming to tell us the great news: Péronnelle is in heat! We welcome her more coolly than her situation demands. Péronnelle is in heat every month and there are not many tomcats in the vicinity.

With immodest gaiety she abandons herself in front of us to ancient dances, of which she observes every rite. She is delightful, striped like a serpent, her fawn underbelly marked with four rows of black dots, velvet buttons fastening her coat, which is in perfect taste.

Three times, her neck outstretched, her eyes eager, she has distinctly called out, in three syllables: *Mi-ya-oo!"* A sacred call followed by birdlike cries, not so easy to write down and interpret. Then follows a serpentine dance; she rolls with abandonment to left and right, and like patients at La Salpêtrière she balances on her neck and raises her body in the air.

Then, up on all fours again, she looks questioningly at the horizon, and her neck swells as she emits the whining of a calf, the sound so low, so loud and out of proportion that Annie opens her eyes and smiles.

Entr'acte: a sacred dance. . . . But since after all the tomcat's presence was not imminent, the sunshine is penetrating, the summer has come back, the acacia leaves are tempting in their heavy flight, Péronnelle leaps up, her tail swinging to the side, steps out the remainder of the rites, looks at us with crazy goatlike eyes which fill her entire face, and rushes after a thistle seed which is journeying through the air. She plays, in a brutal, precise, easily irritable way, interrupting her game now and then with rapid little cat barks: "*Mooek, mooek!*"

"Annie . . ."

"Yes, what is it?"

"Péronnelle . . . this love dance, these dancing-girl contortions—doesn't that remind you of anything?"

Earnestly, she sought her brown hands in the pockets of her tidy little housewife's apron. Her low-dressed hair, hanging heavily over her arched eyebrows, gave her the unbearably touching air of some middle-class Cinderella.

"Come on, Annie, I can see you fairly easily, lying

across the bed in some foreign hotel, cooing, arching your back . . ."

The most daring tricks are always successful! Annie rose to the bait I offered her.

"Oh, come now, I didn't make as much noise as that, Claudine!"

Such modesty! Those hands pushing away the image of sin! If I hadn't learned to know Annie since the other evening, I'd be taken in. If only she'd talk! If only she'd talk! It's the one slightly guilty pleasure she can offer me.

"So it was silent ecstasy, then?"

She turned her shoulders away uneasily: "Listen, Claudine, when it's broad daylight and the sun's shining, I don't know how you can talk so easily about . . . that!"

"Do you find it more natural to *do* it?"

She picked up a cherry left over from the summer, a little skeleton fruit that still had a dry stone in it. Lowering her Chinese eyebrows, she reflected. She was serious and full of concentration, as she nearly always was.

"Yes," she admitted at last. "More natural, and easier too."

I felt I was not going to be bored. In order to see Annie more clearly I pushed my short hair back from my forehead, with a gesture that has almost become a nervous tic. The day was so beautiful it made me sad; the ground grew warm beneath my back. The sun changed color, grew as pink, behind the pine trees, as a beautiful preserving pan. Péronnelle had fallen asleep from exhaustion, and the watchful, ineffective Toby was trying to dig a rabbit hole: he would be at it for a good half hour.

"Explain yourself, Annie!"

"It's not easy, Claudine. But if there's any one thing I cling to in this world, it's you. I don't want to make myself look too small in your eyes. In the days when I saw *people*—Marthe, my brother-in-law, Maugis, my husband—they thought I was stupid. I'm not stupid, Claudine; I'm slightly silly. It's not the same thing at all. A bit of a silly-billy, that's the way to put it. Whenever I want to do something, or just to talk, a peculiar type of anemia makes everything too heavy for me, but I do think, Claudine. I've been thinking and living especially ever since—well, since—"

"Since Baden-Baden, I imagine? Michel Provins said it in delicate terms: 'It's not their own fault if women feel . . .'"

"And I know very well, now, that the woman who's least protected, the one who gives in the most quickly and the most easily, is the most timid, the most silent, the one who offers neither her shoulder nor her knee to the flirtatious hand, the one who is least conscious of wrongdoing, you understand! She lowers her eyes, she barely answers, she keeps her feet under her chair. She doesn't even realize that anything could happen. Only, if someone places a hand on her forehead to push her backward and sees the expression in her eyes, she's lost. She falls through unawareness of herself, through fear, through fear of being laughed at—yes, Claudine!—and also because she wants it to be over, so that she needn't defend herself any longer; she has the confused notion that by giving way she'll find peace and quiet again immediately afterward. Only it can happen that in committing sin she sees the aim and purpose of life, and then . . ."

She fell silent, breathing rapidly, and her eyelids fluttered in an unconsciously theatrical gesture; she lowered her thick eyelashes suddenly, allowing me to sense the magnificence of her face during love-making, a chaste and satisfied expression, a religious bracing of her slim shoulders. . . . Oh, how many pearls she has cast to all those swine!

"If I understand you right, Annie, you don't attach much importance to free will, choice, the vow of monogamy?"

"I don't know," she said impatiently, "I'm explaining something I know, that's all. I realize that women like you or my sister-in-law Marthe—"

"Thanks for the comparison!"

"—go through life as the equals of men, with a kind of aggressive logic and irony, a reasoning flightiness which preserves them from many lapses. For you—for Marthe, for lots of women, the need to reply, *verbally,* in any way to a man's desire, the instinct to indulge in word play, to protest, to simper, if only to cry *no!* gives you the necessary time to think, to save yourselves, in fact. Women like us," concluded Annie, using a mysterious plural, "are women whose defenses have been forgotten."

I was about to reply impetuously, "Then you don't interest me!" But I restrained myself in time: I'm not cruel enough to disturb this little unhinged brain which boasts so innocently of "thinking." And what would be the point? She had learned sexual pleasure without love, she had fallen without nobility, and in spite of what she told me the other evening, without feeling any humiliation. I've no right to tell her this, I who once made her take the easy road, follow a path covered with smooth mud which hinders the step, I can't tell her, "We're certainly not alike, but we're more different than you think. There's something you haven't thought of—it's love! As for me, love has made me so happy, so deeply satisfied physically, so emotionally excited; love, with all its irremediable and precious melancholy, that I really don't know how you can live close to me without dying of jealousy!"

I've no right to break her heart like that. She was lying half-stretched out beside me, smiling inwardly and satisfied with her memories. She stretched, not from laziness, but just as cats flex their muscles before leaping.

"Claudine," she murmured, "I can only remember

63

one afternoon like this. It was in the country at—at —where was it now?—at Agay. Agay is down in the south, near Saint-Raphael, blue and gold like an attractive poster, beside the sea which isn't sea, which hardly moves and curls up asleep in the bays. I'd rented a little villa because of its big garden. And there was nobody there, you see, in December! Maurice Donnay and Polaire hadn't arrived yet."

"Were you there on your own?"

"Of course not. I'd been weak-minded enough— oh, that was the reason, I realize—to take for a fortnight a young man, a very young man—"

"Do I know him?"

"I don't think so. He was a chauffeur. I'd met him at Monte Carlo, where I'd just spent a quiet week at the Riviera Palace . . ."

"But that hotel claims in its prospectus that it's the most *luxuriantly* furnished hotel in Europe! But go on: the young chauffeur—"

"He'd been sacked because his passengers had been thrown out of the car on the Corniche—on the right side, fortunately. Just imagine, he was weeping! So I'd taken him along with me for a fortnight just until he found another job."

"Did he—er—*drive?*"

"He drove," replied Annie briefly. "But he had no moderation. You know, Claudine, people are always saying that the working classes are becoming demoralized, everything's falling apart, and so on. That boy was honesty itself! He had a special kind of tact, it was quite laughable. Believe it or not, at dinnertime, he brought me a louis!"

"What do you mean, a louis? Had he picked it up on the ground?"

"Not on the ground. A 'good class' lady had engaged him by the hour, without any car, and he brought her louis back to me 'for the joint fund' he said."

"It is enough to bring tears to the eyes. What was this hero's name, Annie?"

"Anthelme. As for his surname, my goodness"— her hand went up in the air, its fingers outspread, indicating her forgetful indifference—"it's terribly difficult remembering names, you know! In fact, he was a delightful young creature, a typical Paris boy. He had a way of pronouncing 'matriss,' 'pianna,' he had a way of giving very crude, odd new names to things and actions that you don't usually refer to, at least not out loud. He described them naïvely and made coarse words sound attractive. I assure you . . . one especially that he used to repeat for no particular reason, meaning more or less: 'Don't count on me!' Oh, how silly, I can't remember his name anymore!"

"Don't try, Annie!"

"In any case, it's not important. One afternoon— in the garden—oh, the silence! No flowers on the mimosa, the oranges were green, the yuccas prickly, a glimpse of the sea between the purple rocks . . . he'd been bathing and was drying off without any dressing gown on the sandy terrace . . . I can still see his pink body in the shade of a pine tree . . ."

I smiled, looking at my bare hands, which the shadow of a silvery pine covered at this very moment with a trellis of bluish canvas.

"You know, Claudine, how those young fair-skinned bodies, which don't last very long, are a feast for the eyes and the hands . . ."

"No, I don't know," I said drily in spite of myself.

She put her arm round my waist. She went on, unconsciously caressing and full of pity: "You don't know . . ."

Then her gaze stripped away the damp veil of the sensual mirage and became once again friendly and pure.

"Claudine, may God preserve you from that temptation then!"

"What temptation?" I said with aggressive rigidity.

"Young bodies," she whispered mysteriously.

I shrugged. "Don't worry, Annie! Temptation for me? I've got everything."

"You haven't got everything."

With the tip of a hazel twig she poked at the tunnel dug out by a mole cricket and seemed to be absorbed. She didn't raise her head for fear of losing the courage to say everything. Little ostrich! Has she only to screen her hand with her face and tuck up her skirts in order to reveal her thoughts or her little warm brown body? I laughed in the hope of encouraging her:

" 'I have everything. You have not got everything. He or she has something. The knife of my aunt is less beautiful than the horse of my cousin. The bird has eaten the soldier's pen . . .' It's the beginning of the Ollendorff grammar! Your turn, Annie!"

She was looking down and didn't reply immediately. I could only see her nose, her beautiful animal eyelashes, the corners of her plaintive mouth, which always looks as though she's on the verge of tears.

"Listen, Claudine. I know you're fond of me. But since the other evening, when I allowed myself to tell you everything, I have felt that you don't think much of me and the lot I've chosen. It's a very mediocre share of happiness, but I'd like—I'd like you to share the conviction that each one of us has only a very small portion of happiness, and that is all we ought to have. Even you, Claudine. You carry yours about with a kind of pride, a sort of silent superiority; I can hear what you're thinking: *My happiness or my sorrow, or my pleasure, my love in fact, are better, different from those of other people. . . . Even in what's bad, everything I feel is better!* Forgive me; my summary's a little harsh, but it's for the sake of speed. That's how you see it. Now, I've been thinking about it—I've plenty of time for thinking—and I find it's not like that! I find you're unaware of all that you're missing, probably needing. Love isn't just this—this passionate daughterly feeling that links you to Renaud; it's not this voluntary dependence in which you're living, it's not this serious affection that Renaud pours out to you, affection that grows slowly and exquisitely purer—those were your very words!" she protested, in answer to my gesture. "You've thought about everything," Annie went on, her voice trembling from her own audacity, "except the other kinds of love which occur alongside yours, which can elbow too closely against it, push up to it roughly and say, 'Stand back a bit, we want some room!' I'm still saying 'love,' Claudine, because that's the only word there is. . . . And what if one day you meet mine, that impetuous little demigod, all gleaming with youth, who has rough hands and the low forehead I like, with thick hair? You can hardly ask him for purified tenderness! He throws you down without ceremony, he's only vain about his body, his muscles, his brazen strength, and the only rest you have in his company is when he's asleep, with his obstinate expression, knitted brows, and clenched fists. Then you've got a little time to admire him and wait for him."

Obviously I was very much below par the day before yesterday. Annie's impossible! What wariness on my part, what inadequacy; instead of replying to her sharply and hitting her if necessary, I was reduced to laughing stupidly, all at once, at a leap by the cat? I should have —oh, I'm disgusted with myself, after that little tirade which made her deserve . . . You're getting old, Claudine! But at the same time, why must my better half be away? She was boasting about "thinking." In fact, I'm beginning to believe her.

"My better half" wrote me a strange letter this morning. I can sense that he must have had a dream the night before that showed me in a bad light, and

69

I see nothing good in this. When his dreams drag on like this throughout the day, like a lingering shred of wispy fog, I become anxious. Across the distance I can see the sighs that interrupt his uneasy sleep and the slight convulsions which make his right hand tremble from time to time, a minor St. Vitus' dance suffered by an overworked writer. . . .

He'd dreamt that I was being unfaithful to him, poor dear darling! He's ashamed to tell me about it, ashamed to have dreamt about it, but he easily confuses dream and presentiment, like a milliner in love.

"You realize, Claudine, I'm unhappy because I'm old . . ." Oh, that same old story which touches me and makes me laugh. "My little girl, reassure me. You have a kind of honesty which always convinces me, and I'm sure you'd tell me about it, if you were being unfaithful. . . . It would be *very* wicked of you to say deep down inside yourself: 'I'm deceiving him, but I daren't tell him, it would make him too unhappy.' Isn't that true? if you wanted someone, you'd come and ask me: 'Give him to me!' And I'd give him to you, though I'd be ready to make him die a thousand deaths afterwards . . ."

My poor Renaud! He must have written while still disturbed by an ugly image, anxious and lost in his room with its gleaming walls. I only hope that my reply can retain enough of what I wanted to put into it, the reply I'd like to have written in cheerful orange-colored ink, or with the tip of a burning piece of straw, with the tip of a pink and black firebrand, on a sheet of warm velvety paper resembling my skin. . . . One should be able to draw or paint love letters, or shout them out aloud. If only he reads my expression in it!

I haven't mentioned Marcel to him, naturally. It would have been a bad moment. I want to keep small stumbling blocks like that out of his way: whatever happens, his convalescence mustn't be upset.

The kindhearted Annie's getting a room ready for Marcel next to my *cabinet de toilette,* a room which will please my stepson, for thanks to the Anglomania of Alain Samzun ("my former husband," Annie calls him) our bedrooms are furnished with that bright red mahogany and silvery citronwood with which Waring and Gillow flooded the continent. I don't complain about it, at least not here: the mold-green and trout-blue colors of my living quarters bring through to my side of the windows the iridescent twilight which comes down in the evening over this modest mountain amphitheater.

Marcel's pretty little face will be sheltered—not

long, I hope—beneath gray and pink bed curtains, and he'll powder himself, O Beardsley, at a dressing table with garlands and cabriole feet. I still can't reconcile myself to the fact of his threatened arrival.

"Now, Annie, wasn't it quieter for the two of us, taking life easy, talking about love and travel, picking up pine cones and going slowly along the walks as we did today? Look at that yellow pathway, how it curves suddenly into the undergrowth there; it's like a snake twisting along quickly in search of somewhere cool."

Annie smiled at the calm landscape like someone smiling at indifferent friends. She must feel, deep down, that it lacks men. . . .

"Doesn't Marcel's unexplained visit put you out, Annie?"

She replied with a condescending little pout, a movement of her head vaguely indicating "no." For the ephemeral St. Martin's summer we'd taken out our manila cloche hats again: they were like huge scorched pancakes, and as the big straw brim flapped around her low-dressed hair, she looked like her grandmother must have looked in about 1840. . . .

In front of us Toby-dog was hunting in a vague, inoffensive way for rabbits, tits, moles, and crickets. His broad cleft tongue set off his shiny black coat with the color of heather pink. Because of the returning heat, and also because we'd come out without knowing how far our idleness would lead us, Toby was running about without his collar, naked so to speak, like any bohemian. It was deliciously warm, but the mere sound of the russet leaves in the wind, dried-up brittle leaves, warned me that the summer was over.

"What shall we do with him, Annie?"

"With whom?"

"Marcel, of course!"

She spread out her hands gently and arched her delicate eyebrows.

"We'll do nothing, my dear! How odd you are! You're getting as agitated about your stepson's coming as though it were terribly unpleasant for you—or pleasant!"

"Oh yes, that's it!—Annie, you're upsetting me. Just think, I've found a delightful place where I can endure Renaud's absence in the best way possible, and there are things here I treasure beyond all else, a friend who makes no fuss, a square little bull terrier with the heart of a child, an imperious, distinguished gray cat, and suddenly into all this comes my stepson who uses silk handkerchiefs to blow his nose with! In the first place, it's all your fault!"

"My fault!"

"Of course it is. If only you'd said, 'My goodness, there aren't any real reception rooms in my house . . . my migraine attacks have made me give up social life,' then everything would have been all right!"

"And Marcel would write to your husband!"

"Not necessarily. Shall we go into *Le Bout du Monde*? I'm thirsty."

Le Bout du Monde is well named—a dreary inn squeezed in between two rocks, each a hundred and fifty feet high. A waterfall pours steeply down from the summit, a white thread, apparently motionless and barely pulsating, breaking into a frothing foam in the depths of a gleaming flooded basin. The innkeeper is a poor sniffly creature who lives there in the icy darkness. In summer there are wooden benches at the foot of the waterfall and people going past stop to drink beer and lemonade. When I first went there I looked up at the spray of frosty white water and cried, "How lovely it is!" The innkeeper corrected me:

"It's convenient, rather."

"Oh?"

"Madame wouldn't believe how cool the beer keeps under the waterfall. That's what makes our reputation."

He's here, he's here!
The old horse Polisson hauled up a fine leather trunk,
the gate squeaked in malevolent fashion, Toby
barked, St. Péronnelle-Stylites took refuge on the
sundial, and Annie—I saw her with my own eyes!
—condescended to run. I want to go away: there's
too much bustle in the house.

Yet what a wretched creature I brought back from
the station! A drained, pallid, hollow-cheeked Marcel
with big, anxious eyes, leapt toward me. "Oh my
poor dear!" he exclaimed, in such heartbroken tones
that for a moment I trembled for Renaud and for
myself. Fortunately my stepson's flustered chatter
reassured me:

"My poor dear! I'm done for, I'm fed up, I've been swindled, not a penny left, couldn't go back to my place anymore, nor yours. I've been followed, black-mailed, cheated . . ."

I interrupted him drily: "All very nice, this little word game! But will you tell me precisely what you're talking about?"

He raised his transparent hands.

"Oh, Claudine, I can't *think*, you know! You'll soon understand the whole thing. In the first place, nobody would have thought he was a little crook."

"Oh, he was a little crook, was he?"

"Worse than that, my dear! A pack of them! Three times, do you hear, three times, they stopped me in the street and went through my pockets—and black-mailed me with letters! And threatened me with a revolver! And that horrid little guttersnipe who told me stories with tears in his eyes, like a schoolgirl who's been raped! And the police! And everything else!"

"A nasty business, my boy!"

"It certainly was! In the end they wanted a packet of money, three thousand—they promised to leave me in peace. You refused me, and well . . . that's why I'm here! Just imagine, I nearly missed the train. I had to be as cautious as a thief!"

"You can thank Annie, you know."

"Oh yes! And you too, in spite of the three thousand. You look wonderfully well, Claudine."

77

He took out a pocket mirror and peered at one of his eyes.

"For goodness' sake!" I burst out. "Aren't you going to ask me how your father is?"

A forced smile glimmered on Marcel's face.

"Oh, I'm sure that if he'd had any relapse you'd have told me about him right away."

He yawned, went suddenly pale and leaned against the table.

"What's the matter? Are you going to faint?"

"I don't know," he stammered. "I'm so tired. If I could have some bouillon and a bed . . ."

From that day he's been sleeping—there's nothing else to record. He's been sleeping. He wakes up to eat, drink, ask the time—and then goes to sleep again. I wrote to Renaud:

"Marcel has kindly called in to see us at Casamène. Don't worry, dearest; he's well, he's living a quiet life and isn't in need of money . . ."

I didn't tell the whole truth: Marcel would try the patience of a saint. At first I was worried about his trancelike lethargy and asked the doctor from the little town for his opinion; old Lebon, a plump, complaining, asthmatic man, got his carriage to bring him to the top of our terrible hill and discoursed about his own problems, consisting of depression, suffocation, and catarrh, so I had to fortify him at once with a hot toddy. As a result he consented to take my stepson's pulse, examine his tongue and his delicate skin.

"Could it be some adolescent fever?" he asked doubtfully.

This splendid diagnosis cost me ten francs, but I don't regret the money.

Punctually, three times a day, I climb the single flight of stairs, go down the corridor which smells like a hayloft, knock on the door, and go in without receiving any reply; Marcel is there, sprawling in the shade of the curtains. I can just see a white face with a streak of overlong blond hair across it, a limp hand and hot fingers dangling from his sleeve while his sky-blue silk pajamas gape open over his chest. If he's asleep I put down a cup of consommé and go out, without bothering to walk quietly.

Sometimes a moaning yawn or an inarticulate call keeps me back and I agree to stay for a moment.

"Is that you . . . er . . ."

"No, it's me."

"Oh, it's you, Claudine. What time is it?"

"A quarter to."

"Already! What a sleep I've had! I'm just desperate for sleep. What have you brought me?"

"Red currant jelly and a wing of cold chicken."

"That's nice . . . but I'd like some warm water first. Thank you. How is Annie? Give her my apologies. What's the date today?"

"The seventeenth."

"You're too kind. Good night, Claudine."

And I go down again, relieved for a few hours of my stepmotherly duties. A fine situation for me, between Renaud in the ice house and his son in a state of death trance! Heaven certainly didn't want to endow me with the soul of a sister of mercy. Invalids make me depressed and angry, children irritate me. What a nice nature! I deserve a whole tribe of kids to punish me, all waiting to have their clothes fastened, their noses blown, and their hair combed. . . .

Me have a child! I wouldn't know what to do with it. If I produced one, it would certainly have to be an animal baby with rough hair and tiger stripes, soft paws and hard claws, ears well set and horizontal eyes, like its mother. And Bostock would build us a golden bridge.

My dear Annie has been having a hard time just lately, ever since Marcel's been here. I love to be handled with kid gloves. I only speak to her to tease her or to humiliate her—and what's more, she tolerates it with secret enjoyment. In fact I don't find it difficult to imagine this would-be fugitive in one of those countries where women are yoked to the carriages along with the dogs, while the men stand idly by, singing a song in praise of love, vengeance, and Damascus blades.

In the evening she embroiders or reads. I read or I play with the fire, for it's cold now—a splendid fire of apple-tree stumps, pine cones, and all the springtime prunings: slender branches taken down when the apricot trees were cut back, bundles of lilac twigs which the flame seems to drink up. I shake the brazier, I work the bellows with their flaking Martin varnish, I choose the logs in the box as one chooses favorite books, selecting only the gnarled, colossal ones I can stand on end in the fireplace. At the same time I maintain the sulky silence of a prisoner.

The little tinkling sound of a spoon against porcelain tells me that Marcel's ten o'clock lime tea's being taken up to him, and all at once I clench my teeth, I'm on the point of getting up, sweeping away the lamp, the table, Annie and Marcel, and shouting "Get out! I want to be alone and not hear people living such pointless lives close by me!"

But it's not done. And then they'd be frightened and ask why. Always explanations, always explanations! People are extraordinary: they wouldn't dare ask you about your bodily functions, but they question you bluntly about the reasons for your actions, without shame, without reticence. . . .

"Marthe asks me to give you best wishes," said Annie, folding up a letter.

"Marthe? Marthe Payet? Have you kept in touch with your sister-in-law since your divorce?"

The morning chocolate was steaming between the two of us, and the stove was roaring. In spite of the hard-backed English chairs, the maple dressers, and the Kirby nickel, the long dining room has remained provincial, thank goodness, rather dark and somber: only one window and lots of cupboards for liqueurs, groceries and preserves. The former inhabitants must have eaten there copiously, with devotion. We seem very small in such a room, Annie in a blue dressing gown, I in pink wool with kimono sleeves, my hair untidy but my mind clear, for morning fills my healthy being with bustling cheerfulness again, and as I sit down gaily to table I'm full of appetite for a day that's hardly begun.

The chocolate smells good, the silvery sunlight shines into my cup, Renaud's making good progress, and in his letter he's planning journeys, a dash to the sun, selfish indulgences for the two of us on our own. . . . Morning's a good time! And Annie, as she folds up her letter, is full of remorse for having had such a long tongue!

"Do you correspond with Marthe? I thought you'd quarreled?"

"We did; but two years ago, while I was passing through Paris, we met by accident. I was going to go by without saying a word, but she rushed over to me with a lively show of affection; she told me she'd always been fond of me and that far from blaming me she'd thought I was right to leave him standing, that 'pretentious idiot'—that's what Marthe called him—the man who was my husband and still is her brother. To be honest, I think he'd just refused to give her a certain sum of money which she needed at that moment . . ."

"Which you gave her after that touching little scene of reconciliation!"

"Yes, how did you know?"

"I guessed, my dear: I have a gift for that sort of thing."

"In fact, she paid me back very soon afterwards—"

"Really? Now I find that more surprising!"

"It was about then that she got to know someone who loads her with jewelry, lace, everything."

"But what about Maugis?"

"She keeps Maugis to have rows with, from what she says."

"And what about her husband?"

Annie screwed up an envelope with an embarrassed air.

"Oh, that's not the best part of the story. Poor Léon's unhappy, so unhappy that he's beginning to have talent!"

"You don't say?"

"I don't say, in fact. But haven't you read his last novel, then, *Une femme*?"

"I haven't, actually. He sent it to me, but as I couldn't imagine it would be any less boring than his earlier ones, I didn't even cut the pages."

"Read it, Claudine. You'll see; it's the journal, and a very naïve one, of a man who enjoys his own grief. His friends have said it's shocking, and now poor Léon is regarded as a skeptic, a wretched creature with genius . . ."

"I don't pity him. If you only have to be a deceived husband to have talent . . . your husband would be a literary mandarin, Annie!"

She was laughing like a schoolgirl, her heavy plait

pulling her head backward, when a door opened—and Marcel appeared!

Marcel, in white flannel, stood stockstill like a timid girl bather about to put one foot in the water. Annie stopped laughing at once, her plaintive mouth half-open. I was suddenly angry.

"That's not funny," I shouted. "My boy, you'd better go back to bed at once. I'm fed up with seeing you on the point of collapse and lying on the carpet like a stricken flower!"

Annie, afraid the blood would flow, intervened.

"Not at all! Since you've come down, Marcel, take that chair, the one with its back to the stove. You haven't had breakfast?"

The "stricken flower" smiled dolefully.

"Thank you. What apologies I owe you, and what an unhoped-for refuge I've found with you, my dear Annie!"

His dear Annie! Is he going to speak to her even more intimately then? Really, if I knew that the cellar wasn't too damp, how I'd enjoy locking up this—this Marcel in it!

He sat down, buttered slices of toast, ate them, filled his cup and stirred it, extending his little finger as he held the spoon, and let the sunshine glare blindly into his wide-open eyes, which looked startled and happy.

His ten days in bed, ten days of sleep, chicken, and preserves, have taken ten years off him. He's the adolescent Marcel I knew before my marriage; I would touch his cheek in astonishment to "see if it was real," and look at the tip of my finger afterwards, surprised not to find a trace of silvery pastel powder on it, mingled with the greenish blue used for drawing veins. . . . Is he the same age as me, this bauble? All the sunshine of summer has been reflected from the gold of my skin, it has put gloves on my dry, warm hands and this week's cold wind has made the well-shaped curve of my upper lip smart from slight chapping.

Annie contemplated Marcel with feelings very different from mine, and summed them up in a naïve exclamation.

"It's so amusing to see a man here!"

The "man's" mouth twisted into a pout which expressed everything: vanity, vexation, and the modesty of someone who didn't hope for so much. His slight illness had left him with two little valleys of mauve mother-of-pearl beneath his eyes, too poetic and voluptuous. Annie had stopped eating. Was she thinking, in the presence of my stepson, of the little chauffeur at Agay or the Carlsbad page boy? She had only too much to remember. My goodness, how I'd laugh if she fell in love with Marcel! Beggars can't be choosers. . . . But I know him. He won't let himself be caught—how shall I put it?—he'll always slip away.

"Is Father well, Claudine?"

"He's not too bad, thank you. He writes to me three times a week."

"Will he be coming back soon?"

"I don't know. The doctors say he's more stimulated by the altitude than really cured. Three weeks, a month, perhaps more . . ."

"What a long time it's taking!" exclaimed Marcel politely.

"You're right!"

"Oh, overwork, my dear! So I . . . but I don't want to bore Annie."

"Not at all, not at all . . ."

"And in any case, I'm cured! You're my two angels!"

"Yes, we know, we know. . . . When are you leaving?"

The delicate pink faded from his cheeks! He cast a timid glance toward the door. I felt slightly ashamed.

"I mean, there's nothing to take you back to Paris, or anywhere else?"

"Would it be wise . . ." Annie began.

She didn't finish her sentence, but I was aware of the indirect reproach. My goodness, she knows about life! Annie wouldn't settle down in a friend's house and organize animals and people, change the mealtimes, and disturb the apathy of a lazy farmer who was letting forgotten potatoes rot in the ground.

No, I'll keep silence. And that will be even worse. They can shiver in their shoes, for I'm going to be polite and impersonal. . . . A vain resolution: You have to learn that sort of thing when you're very young. . . .

The silence began to weigh upon us: Annie was uncomfortable and Marcel was scratching away at the ecru tablecloth. I was hypnotized by the star shape that was cut out in the stove door. Finally my dark-skinned friend took a deep breath and repeated faintly like an unhurried echo:

"I assume there's nothing to take you back to Paris?"

"No, nothing. On the contrary, in fact . . ."

I uttered a coarse laugh. Oh, yes, "on the contrary." He's terrified of being robbed or worse still. What a pitiful creature!

"So you'll do us the honor of staying some time?"

There's nothing special about that little remark. But when Annie says it, it's no more and no less than a show of strength, a show of independence, an act of lèse-Claudine!

Marcel, who's more intelligent than she, was aware of this. And it's me that he looked at, as he replied, hesitatingly:

"You're terribly kind, Annie . . . but . . ."

"Stay, Marcel, don't make such a fuss."

I placed my hand on her shoulder in a caress that

was more of a blow, and as an unsociable hostess my *amour propre* was satisfied as I felt this sloping shoulder, graceful, feminine, and very much Second Empire, yield beneath my firm grasp.

Life is getting organized for the three of us, and it's less difficult than I'd feared. And then Renaud writes me such reassuring letters, full of warm recognition that I don't deserve! "I was sure of you, my darling, I knew you'd sort everything out, that you'd smooth my pillow, and you've drawn to 'Port-Annie' the lost child I've brought up so badly . . ."

In return for that letter, that cry of gratitude I hardly deserved, I wanted to weep tears of shame, break the windows, and ruin the English furniture by kicking it. Only Toby knew; the little black gnome lying under the table sensed the first onset of the destructive force. His body trembled as he rose anxiously on his short hind legs, holding his outlandish face with its eyes of jet and gleaming teeth on a level with the table, his square claws like those of some well-meaning demon emerging from the abyss. Then I stroked him and silently asked his forgiveness.

Yes, life is getting organized; I try to organize it in my own way, and I often fail. Between Annie and Marcel, who hardly exchange a word when I'm not there, I sense the kind of secret alliance you get between the weak and the crafty. My stepson, who's an expert in the art of calculating his effects, gradually displays a range of ties, flat caps with large peaks, knickers, and Tyrolean stockings designed to drive a crowd wild with excitement. There's a certain Norfolk suit—again a little too tight—in which he acts the part of a page. Annie is so thrilled that she even replaits her black pony tail three times a day.

I despise all this and don't condescend to get out of my short homespun skirts or the warm soft tunic shirts in plain bright orange, Chinese pink, and turquoise green which enhance my looks and make pleasant splashes of color on the rusty lawns. Rough wool on top and splendid fine linen underneath—I can't think of any greater physical happiness in the world. Marcel laughs and calls me "daughter of the Mevas brood," which gets my back up. The Mevas, who sleep on planks of wood and eat raw parsnips, are dangerous idiots. Raw parsnips! Oh the breath of some sweet Meva bride. . . .

However, my people (my little unhinged girl and my young pervert), my people, if they're not murmuring, are becoming evasive; something's changed in my peaceful little hilly kingdom, my cabachon where the traces of a pretentious civilization are slowly fading away. For instance. . . .

"What are we doing today, Claudine?"

"I don't know about *you*, Marcel; as for me, *I'm* collecting pine cones and mushrooms too, perhaps. What about you, Annie?"

"Me? nothing . . . I don't know."

"Having arranged the program for the holidays . . . goodbye, children. I'm busy until I hear the bell for lunch."

Then I went off in an affected way, with a basket on each arm and Toby in walking dress. Toby's walking dress consists mainly of an apple which he carries in his mouth, and as the apple's too big it distends his jaws and makes him look like a dolphin. It obviously bores him to death, but he must have made a vow.

After I'd gone about fifty yards Marcel ran along and caught up with me.

"Where are the pine cones?"

"Under the pine trees."

"Are they far away?"

"In that little wood, on the other side of the valley."

"I'll come with you."

"If you wish."

I whistled as I walked rapidly through the wet grass.

Marcel looked regretfully at his shiny little yellow boots, hesitated and followed me. Under the pine trees it was dark, as though a storm was brewing, and there was a hushed silence anticipating gusts of wind. The scent of pine cones, rotting leaves, and newly grown mushrooms made me feel fifteen years younger; I see myself at Montigny with my foster sister Claire—the flock of sheep is over there, on the other side of the wood, and we'll light a fire of twigs and roast apples in the ashes. . . .

"What's that you're singing, Claudine?"

"A song from the time when I was little . . ."

A song that comes from far away, from Montigny-en-Fresnois . . . I can still hear my rough young voice . . . a song that dates from before my life, from before Renaud, from before love. . . . Oh, how I love my childhood!

> *Hé, n'querriez donc point, ma Mère,*
> *Y vins de Dijon,*
> *De vouer passer la bannière*
> *Du princ' de Borbon . . .*

I picked up pine cones in busy, forgetful silence; my fingers grew sticky with aromatic resin and finally I stood up, my back bent.

"I say, Marcel, don't wear yourself out!"

His crafty chin jutted forward, and his blue eyes, which looked dark under the peaked cap, watched me with childish malice.

"You don't think I'm going to put my hands in all that mess!"

"It's not a mess, it's resin."

He bent down, picked up a dry pine cone by one scale, holding it between two fingernails, and threw it into the basket, stretching out his arm like a little girl throwing stones.

"There, I've done enough. . . . Oh, here's Annie!"

It was Annie in fact. Wearing a red linen beach cape tied under her chin, she was walking slowly along in idle fashion and purposely exaggerated her absentminded gaze in order to say, "I wasn't coming to join you. I happened to be passing."

"Annie!"

A mocking echo answered us from the valley, faint but distinct. She replied from a long way off: "Claudine!" but no concealed "double" repeated her call. I sat down on a carpet lined with pine needles and carefully peeled a young mushroom that was covered with grass as fine as hair. It was moist and cold, as pearly and tender as a lamb's muzzle and so tempting that instead of putting it in the basket I chewed it raw; it was delicious and tasted of truffles and earth.

"What are you eating?" cried my friend.

"Mushrooms."

"Good heavens! She'll poison herself! Marcel, stop her. . . . I've brought the letters," she added.

Why did I interpret this simple remark as a kind of excuse for her arrival? I don't like this theatrical manner of explaining an entrance or an exit. I know I'm very hard to please! People who've only met me three times can be mistaken. When they see me with windswept hair, my skirt down to the ground, my posture upright and my eyes straight in gaze, they say to themselves: "There's the woman for me! Active, lively, and so easy to live with!" You try then! If I were a man and knew myself well, I wouldn't care much for me: unsociable, enthusiastic or hostile at first sight, possessing a flair which claims to be infallible and makes no concessions, full of fads, pseudo-bohemian, very "respectable," in reality jealous, sincere out of laziness and untruthful out of modesty. . . .

I say that today, and then tomorrow I'll find myself delightful.

"I had a letter from Father, Claudine."

"Oh?"

It was a vexatious "Oh?" that escaped my lips. A letter from Renaud which wasn't for me! And that crafty Marcel had been hiding it from me since that morning!

At the end of the corridor which smelled of a country attic and feed store, we were saying good night, holding up our lamps. I raised my arm and purposely let the light shine on Marcel's face, his narrow temples and eyes that were not really blue—they were a slightly subnormal turquoise—the smooth, cruel forehead, the chin broken by an oblong dimple like

97

Rézi's. The long nights of chaste sleep, the mountain air, a few weeks of biting cold and sunshine had been enough to restore a disturbing charm to his entire face. Due to his habitual coquettishness the moist, gleaming lips parted slightly whenever anyone looked at him.

"Do you use face powder, Marcel?"

"I still use a little. You've got such a cutting wind in this place!"

"It's made specially to our requirements. In any case, you look fine!"

"Thanks to you!"

"Tell me—did Renaud say anything special?"

He laughed with an air of amused pity.

"Always the same story! Come in for a moment, then, I'll read it to you."

The pink and gray bedroom smelled of new-mown hay mingled with another more tartish perfume. I hesitated between ecstasy and nausea. I put down my lamp and Marcel generously handed me Renaud's letter. . . . Nice remarks which were more friendly than fatherly, news about the snow, anecdotes about tobogganing, and these touching lines: "Look after Claudine, my boy. She's just as much my child as you are, and I don't know which one of you I should entrust to the other . . ."

I smiled sadly, as I watched Marcel undress. He treated me as a pal more than a stepmother, and removed his clothes slowly, revealing underwear that was—professional. . . .

"By Jove! Those pink silk underpants, my dear! All for Casamène? Lucky Annie!"

"Come on now, don't tease me!" He untied his tie in front of a tall glass and stamped his foot sulkily. "You know very well that it's not for Annie, nor for you. Only you know in what a state of panic I packed my trunk, and—"

"By the way, nobody followed you from there?"

"No, thank goodness!" he sighed, sinking into a deep armchair, comfortably clad in white flannel pajamas. "A nasty business all the same. Schoolboys! I shan't get caught again!"

"But you told me it was a swindler?"

"Yes, but I met the swindler through the schoolboy."

"An odd way of doing it!"

"It's so complicated! Anyway, here's the gist of it. Vaney—you know Vaney—that charming fair-haired boy, with skin as pink as a bonbon?"

"I don't know him."

"You're the only one who doesn't! You run around my father nonstop and you know nothing about the outside world. . . . Well, Vaney, that angel, that plaster saint, my dear, he was in league with the swindler!"

"Oh!"

"He picked up smart chaps through family contacts, and since he didn't dare offer his own favors he found people for the little swindler and shared the proceeds with him. Once they were in the hands of the little swindler and his gang, if I can put it that way, and he was really a bit too young, the chaps were in a tight spot. I'm sorry I'm talking like a schoolboy —I picked it up from Vaney . . ."

"The saintly young girl?"

"He was more like a sacred courtesan!"

"Eh?"

"He was the sacred courtesan at the Lycée Marat when I knew him. Of course, you don't know. Those kids have got a complicated hierarchy; it's like something from Ubu-Roi and Flaubert. I found it amusing for three weeks. Would you believe that they'd decorated me 'as an outsider' with the order of 'Eliphas de Muerdre.' I used to go to the *parloir* on Saturdays . . ."

"What a carry-on and what a mob!"

"Excited little faces at every door, and they would laugh so that I'd condescend to turn around. They'd drop handkerchiefs and brush against my elbow, saying 'Oh, sorry!' They wrote letters, some were anonymous, some signed . . . oh, those were good times! Oh, what it was to be young!"

"Just listen to the old man of eighty!"

He was irritated, wriggled in the depths of his chair and showed undisguised contempt.

"The most intelligent woman—and you are the

most intelligent woman, Claudine!—never understands at first. It's not my youth I'm regretting, it's
theirs! What will become of them, all my charming
little boys? If one of them keeps his smooth white
skin and his slim figure, so many others turn into
coarse young cocks, covered with spots; they look
dirty because they don't shave, they're ashamed of
themselves, and out of sheer stupidity they hide behind kitchen maids' skirts. Their hands grow big,
their voices break, and most of all their noses, oh,
those heartbreaking noses! And hairs growing everywhere and—ugh!—they're young men, if you wish,
they're no longer intoxicating adolescents, with flaw-
less beauty which doesn't last, unfortunately . . .
young bodies . . . !"

"Young bodies . . ." Where had I heard those two
voluptuous words, into which the mouth bites as it
utters them? Oh, yes, Annie. . . . What did she say?
"God preserve you, Claudine, from the temptation of
young bodies! . . . You can't know! . . ." What stupid
young gluttons they both are! Treating love like this,
as though it were something eatable! I'd like to tell
them. . . . But what's the use? I said good night
coolly, in a know-all pompous way to my stepson,
who looked like a slender Pierrot wearing a silk head-
band of blond hair, lying there limply in his white
flannel. . . .

O dear Renaud, how calmly and wisely I shrug my shoulders as I read your letter today! It's concerned (with that attention to detail, so misleading at first about your nature, which is not really very methodical) with planning, month by month, stage by stage, our escape for next summer! "In June we leave Paris for six good weeks in Montigny; at the end of July, Vittel. . . . And then in mid-September we must absolutely fix a little round trip I have in mind toward the Black Forest, something old-fashioned, Second Empire. . . . What do you say to that, darling?"

What do I say? I say yes, naturally. If I said no,

in the first place you'd sulk, then I can see you working out another itinerary, selecting another spa that would be good for your arthritis. And as for my consent! Wherever you like, wherever you like. . . . Since I'm certain of finding with you, through your mere presence, everything I need—sometimes slightly more —I'm indifferent about the future. I walk toward it heedlessly, moving backwards, dragging my feet.

Heedlessly, I didn't say patiently. If you come back later than you said, if I'm thirsty in summer and have to wait a whole long moment for a glass of cool water, if the peach hanging against the wall ripens too slowly, I'm furious, yes. I fly into a rage, and my irritated sigh expresses the mortal weight of an hour that seems interminable, but . . . but that doesn't mean that I'm like you, and what an overprecise arrangement, a year carved up in advance, served in front of me, for twelve months, like an *assiette anglaise!*

What must happen, will happen, and that's that. What am I saying! It's happening already, in spite of you and your careful plan. You're glad that when our *tête-à-tête* reaches its most silent moment, I like neither haste nor . . . big mouthfuls. Be glad that I like easygoing days and don't force me, on the pretext of being farsighted, to enjoy simultaneously both this year and next.

When I was little, a deep, precocious wisdom was

directed toward me when I felt happiest, various melancholy warnings, full of deep bitterness that belonged to an age older than mine. Did the wise words say: "Are you thinking of a beautiful lady in white wearing a diadem, who appeared to me among the dark foliage of the old walnut tree?" Not at all! It was the simple, ordinary "inner voice," a near-painful immobilization of my thought, of the entire healthy little animal that is me, aroused and replete, a half-open door which for children of my age usually remains closed. It said to me, "Look, stop, this moment is beautiful! Is there anywhere else, in your entire bustling existence, a sun so bright, lilac so blue because it's mauve, a book so absorbing, fruit so juicy with scented sweetness, a bed so cool with rough white sheets? Will the shape of these hills ever seem more beautiful to you? How much longer will you be that child intoxicated with her life, with the mere happy throb of her own arteries? Everything within you is so fresh that you don't realize that you have limbs, teeth, eyes, a sweet, perishable mouth. Where will you feel the first bite, the first decline? Oh, try to halt the passage of time, try to remain a little longer something like yourself; don't grow up, don't think, don't suffer! Try, hope so much for this that somewhere a god will be moved at it and grant your wish!"

I confided all this to you one day, Renaud. You

didn't smile at the radiant little thing that I was, but your black, vindictive look penetrated deep into my eyes, the look of absurd and obstinate jealousy, which vexes and delights me as it cries out:

"I forbid you to tell me there was a time when I didn't know you!"

"It's me, Annie. I wonder if you've any—any vaseline, some sort of ointment, or glycerine? It's for my lip, it's chapped and I'm biting it all the time . . ."

Annie opened her bedroom door and stood on the threshold in astonishment, with that plaintive, Chinese look she has when her long black hair has been plaited for the night. I was making excuses and giving explanations, for I hardly ever go into Annie's bedroom. I feel that she doesn't like anyone's presence there, not even mine. Is she afraid that the yellow curtains, the white wallpaper with its frieze of laburnum and the commonplace white furniture, typical of some well-ordered hotel, will recount her restless nights, her state of near-somnambulism? There's no smell of mystery about the bedroom, I'm not aware of any personal scent—at the very most a perfume of exotic, precious wood, emanating, I'd swear to it, from Annie's own body; she uses no artificial scents. . . .

A traveler's room where I expect to see a parchment trunk in one corner . . . the writing table reveals a virgin blotter and a rusty pen. No photograph smiles from the bare wall. The day when my friend goes away again she may take that half-open novel lying on the bed with its turned-down sheets, that little handkerchief screwed up on the table, and nothing of Annie will remain in that impersonal bedroom. . . .

My strange hostess waited, her sad blue eyes wide open in her brown face, and her lips parted as I spoke, with that involuntary pout which makes you want to laugh and smack her. . . .

"Ointment for sore lips? . . . no . . . there's never anything in this house . . . ah, but wait a moment!"

She opened a cupboard, poked about in a vague tangle of things and turned around with satisfaction.

"There. That can be used for chapped skin, I think."

On the box she held out to me I read: "Theatrical Greasepaint, Rachel."

"But—that's the stuff they use on the stage! Where did you pinch that?"

"I didn't pinch it. I bought it because I needed it. It must have gone a bit rancid by now."

"Was it some drawing-room performance?"

"Not at all," she sighed wearily. "Theatrical mime drama. I performed as a mime for a few days."

"Where? Was it abroad?"

I questioned her drily. I was irritated and hurt by everything she hid from me—or did she invent it? She sat down on her bed and pressed her hand over her forehead. I pulled at the bare slender arm which emerged from her pale blue dressing gown.

"Are you teasing me, Annie?"

On feeling that she was being slightly browbeaten she smiled in acquiescence. It was warm; a wood fire had gone out beneath the white fluffy ash. I pushed Annie along with my hip to make room for myself next to her on the padded eiderdown. I was pleased at the thought of the fine story I knew nothing about, at having won Annie's confidence again, at the hour that was already late, and the silky swish of the winter rain against the shutters. . . .

Annie curled up and hugged her knees with her arms.

"Well," she began, "do you remember a sort of variety show at the Théâtre des Pâturins? They put on a little opera in two acts, it was very tragic, called *La Vieille Reine*, and then a *Slice of Life* in which everyone was killed, and then a student farce, and finally a mime drama entitled *Le Dieu, le Mirage et la Puissance!*"

"Er—I remember vaguely."

"I thought you would. The theater went out of business after a fortnight. The mime drama was nice all the same. I played the little slave girl who picks roses and is carried off by the faun at the end."

"You! . . . You've been on the stage?"

She smiled without vanity. "I didn't say that, Claudine. I appeared in mime. It's not difficult, you know! And then, I was pushed into it . . . I must tell you . . ."

She smoothed tiny little pleats into the jabot of her cambric nightdress which hung out of her loose dressing gown.

"I'd just met a 'little play-actor,' as they say. A young man from the Conservatoire, in other words. Oh, it doesn't matter which one! He'd had an honorable mention for tragedy, yes, but unfortunately that didn't make him a tragedian, far from it. He'd played small parts in Sarah's company: Lord Vendramin, the page Orlando, because of his legs, legs that were . . ."

She tried to find a comparison but could find nothing adequate.

"Legs, in fact! One day when he was acting the page Orlando, Sarah said to him: 'My boy, you have the legs of the period.' "

"What period, Annie? Sarah's?"

"No—the sixteenth century, I think . . ."

"Where did you pick him up?"

She laughed in my face, pressed her little clenched fist into the plump pillow and said nothing.

"You're not nice, Annie! Tell me everything or I'll tickle you!"

I said that without thinking, but the effect was astonishing. Annie huddled up against the wall, stretched out her hands toward me in terror and begged: "No, no, not that, it'll kill me! I'll tell everything!"

She stopped suddenly, swallowing her saliva:

"I met him at your place, there!"

"My place? You're making it up! I've never known any Renaissance page. You're out of your mind, Annie."

"Not at all! He was—that poor boy, really—temporary secretary to Renaud for three weeks."

I struck my forehead as they do on the stage:

"Wait now! . . . A boy with too much hair, not enough linen, beautiful eyes . . ."

She indicated agreement, at each phrase, by a nod of her head.

"That's it, that's it! He was called—"

"Auguste," she said in a low voice.

"At our place he called himself simply Monsieur de Saint-Yorre."

"It was a pseudonym."

How nicely she said that! how kindhearted she is!

This is how I like her, the way I would like her to be always, half-silly, half-perverse, utterly tortured with impurity beneath her chaste attitude. I drew her toward me by her thick plait, as though she were a piece of fruit at the end of a flexible branch, and I kissed her just anywhere, on her cheek, on her cold little nose. Poor child! She yields to the slightest caress, she belongs to everyone, to me if I wanted, to Francis the gardener. . . .

"Oh, it was a pseudonym? Come now, darling! And then?"

"Nothing. Nothing . . . at first. You remember that I was in hiding at that period. Alain, Marthe, my divorce case . . . I said good-bye to you and I left again for . . . Casamène, and I wasn't due to go through Paris again until three months later, in May—"

"I remember. But I didn't see you again that year, did I?"

She shrugged her shoulders, raised her eyebrows and her chin. "What could I do? You must forgive me, Claudine. I came back to Paris in May and fate decreed that outside the Hotel Regina I met—"

"Lord Vendramin. Did he appear at a good moment?"

"I couldn't imagine a better moment," sighed Annie. "My trip to London—"

"To Casamène, I thought?"

"No, to London . . . had bored me to death; I was

starved, everything's so carefully supervised there! And then Lord Vendramin looked splendid that day. He was pale, his eyes . . ."

"His legs . . ."

"I only learned why afterwards . . . I was amazed that he didn't greet me at once."

"It's because . . . I'll tell you. Renaud had sacked him because of a little incident—oh, nothing serious —trafficking in theater tickets. He got them out of theater managements in Renaud's name and then sold them. Oh, it goes on all the time, but Renaud didn't like it very much."

I was trying to exculpate Lord Vendramin; I seemed to be making excuses for Renaud. My tact was wasted, for Annie wasn't at all embarrassed and went on:

"Yes, I suspected . . . in any case, I didn't care a bit . . . that same evening I went up to his room with him.

"Well now! really!"

In spite of myself I let go of my friend's warm little hands. I took hold of them again at once; I was afraid I might have hurt her feelings. But she abandoned them to me, limp and soft as they were, and concentrated on her memories:

"A month later I was still with him, Claudine! He wouldn't accept any money from me . . ."

"Fancy!"

"But I paid for everything."

"Oh, fine!"

"Poor dear, he tried to get engagements everywhere and found nothing. At night he didn't think about them anymore. He only thought about me, and I only thought about him."

My laughter was a little forced.

"Oh, Lord Vendramin turned out to be a Hercules, did he?"

"Oh, good heavens, no," she conceded with a delicate little pout. "But something else . . . he had the youthful, frantic viciousness of a town dweller, the schoolboy habit of exhibiting all the physical manifestations of it, even provoking them himself, if necessary. He'd read horrible books and remembered them at every opportunity with a devotion to detail that wasn't really justified."

"And what about you?"

"Me"—she raised her hand rather uncertainly, as though she were drunk—"as for me, I followed his reminiscences and his innovations . . . and I did the paying. But I'm pretty sure that I'm still in his debt."

(Annie had obviously had her money's worth.)

"But what about the theater?"

"Oh yes . . . well, this is what happened. One evening he came to the hotel very late, excited and full of himself. He walked up and down for a full minute before telling me that he'd got an engagement at the Pâturins, in a mime drama. I felt our liaison was coming to an end. All the more so because the rehearsals began immediately and he talked to me enthusiastically about an English girl with long red hair, a young girl from a good background who had run away from her family. "She's wonderful," he would repeat, "she has a marvelous figure, and she has a sense of movement and rhythm too, there's a nobility about her gestures . . ." What hadn't she got, according to him, that Yvée Lester? I was counting the days, Claudine; I was waiting for the première, the end of those rehearsals which took Auguste away from me all day. . . . He would come home tired and absentminded; he would—make love to me in a commonplace way, quickly, without imagination. . . .

"Two days before the première that I was so much looking forward to, Auguste climbed up to my room in a panic. 'Get your hat,' he said; 'you're coming with me.' 'Where?' 'To the Pâturins.' And on the way he told me an extraordinary story: The girl with red hair had been summoned back to her family, she'd gone without a word of excuse, the authors and the manager were in a state of panic. And, since I didn't understand, he added: 'You're taking the part; they'll stick you in a red wig, I'll drum the thing into you for forty-eight hours, and we'll save the show! Do you understand? They'll keep the society girl's name on the posters and get the takings all the same!' Oh, Claudine! I felt I was going out of my mind!"

"Why didn't you say no?"

She gazed at me in astonishment.

"But he wanted me to do it, Claudine! He wanted me to do it! And then, I don't know—once I was there, everybody around me congratulating me before I'd done anything, egging me on, pushing me this way and that, that dark little theater, the three electric light bulbs in the footlights which hypnotized me with their concentrated glare . . . and then Auguste started to pose me on the stage at once, he sang me the bars of music for my entrance . . . I felt drained, torn out of myself, taken over by people who were fighting over my poor little personality. What a drawback it is to be so little in command of oneself!

"That first rehearsal, my God! Before I'd agreed to anything everyone was already treating me like a piece of human furniture. The author called out to me: 'Take your hat off, mademoiselle! They have to see the expression on your face!' 'Lift up your skirt,' shouted Auguste. 'They have to see the movement of your legs! . . .'

"And then Willette Collie, who was playing the Faun, cried out when I arrived: 'Is that the red-haired girl? Go stone the crows!' She leapt about the stage like a demon, wearing a bathing suit, and danced blind, her short hair falling down over her nose. She too got hold of me as though I were a dead animal, a torn garland. . . . Oh, I had no trouble playing my part, right from the first rehearsal! Willette Collie, who had to carry me off at the end of the mime drama, threw me down so roughly, dragged me along with such a convincing air of triumph, and suffocated me with a kiss so well acted that I was nearly reduced to tears. I pleaded with her involuntarily—I scored a success. . . .

"My young friend was triumphant. As a result he forgot to comfort me or to add a word of affection to all the praise that turned my head. He smoked, with his head tilted sideways and one eye closed, pulling an odd face to avoid the smoke which made his eyes smart, without removing his cigarette from his lips. . . .

"For two days I didn't emerge from this hell. What was left of me? What are all those people really made of, they're capable of miming, talking, shouting, hurling vile words at one another?

"Yes, and the next moment, exaggerated compliments . . . I know, I've seen rehearsals. They expend fantastic amounts of energy, they make the same gesture fifteen times over, and gradually it becomes uncluttered and precise, it stands out as something luminous and perfect. I know this mixture of hysterical activity, lazy, idle grumbling, stubborn idiotic vanity, obstinate nobility. They laugh at a silly pun, cry over a wig that turns out wrong, have dinner when they can, and sometimes they sleep. They're bad-tempered, sensitive, angry, puffed up with their own achievements, and then all at once they're kindness itself.

"Oh yes, that's it! Your summary's a caricature, but they're just like that, Claudine . . ."

She fell silent, tucked her chilly feet beneath her and remained in a fatalist attitude of gypsylike immobility, her eyes downcast, her plait on her shoulder. I quickly tightened the slack thread of the fine story:

"And after that, Annie? The first night?"

"The first night? . . ."

She sought for words, concentrating, her eyebrows arched:

"Well, it was like the first two days."

"But what about the audience? Did you have stage-fright? Where you a success?"

"I didn't see the audience," she said simply. "It was pitch dark in front. The glare from the footlights made my head ache. In the depths of that gaping blackness I felt the hot breath and the movement of invisible animals. My head was bursting with fatigue, and my makeup, an English makeup in pale pink, white and periwinkle blue, made the skin on my cheeks feel tight. And the wig, Claudine! My own hair's thick; imagine the weight of wavy, curly red hair, the frizzy mane of some auburn Salome . . . I had to look like the young English girl who's been demanded by her father, the lord. My comrades cried out in admiration when they saw me—but those over-excited creatures make a fuss so easily, you know. A tunic in white crepe de chine, buskins, a basket of roses in my trembling hands, that was all . . ."

"And then what, Annie?"

"Then it happened that I was a big success. It's

true. I went through my new job twenty times, like a sleep-walker, side by side with Auguste, who played the part of a young Athenian. He's the one you should have seen, Claudine! You should have seen his wine-colored tunic, his strong little knees, his feminine ankles and his neck, a powerful neck set on delicate shoulders. We arrived at the theater; I would put on the wig that gave me a headache and . . . it went very well until my big scene with the Faun, Willette Collie. That crazy creature went to a lot of trouble to vary our duo every evening, and I would tremble in advance at the thought of it. One day she grabbed me around the the waist like a parcel and carried me off under her arms, my tunic and my red hair dangling triumphantly behind like a tail. Another time, during our kiss—the famous 'kiss' which caused an uproar, and which she bestowed on me with casual intensity—she slipped her hand under my arm and tickled me unmercifully. My mouth was gagged by hers, but I uttered a little breathless cry . . . I needn't tell you any more! They nearly had to lower the curtain . . . I cried that night."

"Cried, why?"

"Because Auguste, who was waiting for me in the wings, made a terrible scene!"

"I suppose he was jealous?"

"Jealous? . . . Oh no! He simply didn't like 'that kind of joke.' In order to show the others that he knew how to talk to his woman, he threatened me straight out with a real *tourlousine*. Do you know what that is?"

"I can guess."

"But this is what happened. Willette Collie (she was adjusting her horns behind the support) leapt at him like a panther and called him a 'blasted little pimp.' "

"A mere nothing."

"He told her that all those tricks were beginning to get on his nerves."

"Oh, I love that! And then?"

"Then Willette Collie wanted to scratch his eyes out, and on top of that she ran her head into his stomach. Just imagine, with those sharp horns!"

"Was there any bloodshed?"

"No, Claudine, thanks to the intervention of fat old Maugis who happened to be there—"

"Just by chance."

"—he separated them, standing there with his arms outstretched in the same pose as that woman in the foreground of *The Rape of the Sabines,* uttering conciliatory jokes at the same time . . ."

"What a strange man he is, Maugis! By the way, Annie, did the newspapers pay any attention to you?"

"The newspapers, Claudine! They recounted my childhood in an aristocratic cottage, my vocation, which wasn't to be denied, my flight to Paris, my despairing family, and all the time they left me anonymous in a tantalizing way . . ."

Annie raised both her dark little hands toward the ceiling and then fell back tired and silent. She ran a dry tongue over her plaintive mouth, which drooped at the corners. Once again I asked myself if she was experiencing a waking dream or whether she was lying. No, she wasn't lying. She'd experienced everything she was telling me. Her memory was a bumpy road, a steep slope with the dizzy sharp rises of a switchback, scattered with little nude men, young, obscene, of all colors. . . . I was sure she had done everything she told me, and everything she didn't; and all things considered, nothing was simpler and more commonplace than her life, the life of a little animal who'd discovered her sexuality and used it with delight.

Annie was silent. I woke her up.

"And then what, Annie?"

"You always say 'and then what?'! How curious you are, Claudine! And then . . . the performances came to an end, along with my poor little love affair."

"Did he walk out on you?"

"Precisely, Claudine. Sarah took him off on a tour to act the parts of pages who appeared in tights . . ."

"Did you miss him?"

"Not very much. By the end he was beating me."

"Oh!"

Annie moved her shoulders as though she could remember rough treatment.

"When I say he was beating me, I'm probably using

rather strong words. He was such a schoolboy, you know. First of all he would biff me as a joke, instead of jostling me with his shoulder, and then he developed the habit of pinching me while he caressed me; he would spank my bottom and play nasty tricks. No, I wasn't too upset. All that, you know . . .'

She slid down to the end of the bed, revealing a glimpse of her saffron-colored legs against the yellow satin of the eiderdown, and I realized she was indicating that our conversation had come to an end. I picked up my little lamp again.

"All that, Annie?"

She hesitated, then smiled with the embarrassed air of some young lass, and said finally:

"All that, Claudine, doesn't deserve to be considered in any other way. Other people, like you, say: 'Love, oh! . . .' and you add a lot of fine phrases. In my case, my body does the thinking. It's more intelligent than my brain. It reacts more sensitively, more completely than my brain. When my body thinks, that's to say, when I—when he—"

"I understand, I understand!"

"Well, at that moment everything else is silent. At those moments, my whole body has a soul . . ."

When I left her she was standing, her hands clasped low down in front of her body; at what visions of chaste nudity were her limpid eyes gazing?

O charming little body that knows so well how to leave your soul! I'm alone, and I make comparisons between the two of us. I've never studied a woman as much as you, for I instinctively despise my sisters who resemble you, and I have no women friends at all. What about Rézi? But I didn't study Rézi, I looked at her and I desired her. . . . And you can be sure too that she never deserved anything more, or better. She too would talk freely and intimately about sexual pleasure; she would seek it out, she aroused it, or else she would thrust it aside recklessly, she would "put it off" like some delicious morsel which would still be eatable the next day . . . I used to admire her for it with slight distaste. How would I have made her understand me, and how would I make Annie undersand me? I don't seek pleasure, it seeks me, finds me, attacks me and overwhelms me with a hand and mouth so rough that I'm left trembling afterwards. Or else it prowls slowly around me, exhausts me with its invisible approach, while within me pride struggles mutely against it. At this moment of confusion a delectable antagonism intervenes between me and Renaud; it's no longer our faithful love, it's not tender, nor merciful, it clenches its teeth defiantly, muttering: "I'll take you before you take me . . ."

And my blood throbs hotly in my veins because I can hear through the dark air of the night, across the leagues of snow, the voice of the one man who has the right to say to me:

"I'll kill you if any other man but me sees your

eyes, your eyes which fill with resentment at the moment when they owe me the most gratitude!"

For how proud I am when I think of it! He whom so many leagues separate from me, he whom the cold imprisons up there, right up there on top of an unknown mountain, I've changed him, that frivolous Renaud, my young husband with silver hair. I barely admit that it's taken me a long time. We haven't yet attained the physical resemblance which makes an old married couple into a pair of brothers, although I've acquired from Renaud some familiar and feminine gestures, such as raising my little finger, while in return he imitates my obstinate, taurine way of sulking and butting, with my head lowered and my neck working up and down . . . I'm only pleased by the profound and definitive infiltration through which I've Claudinized him. Whatever he does from now on, and whether I'm alive or not, I dwell within him. He came to me slowly, surely, not without defenses and retreats—he came to me utterly.

I've made him less gay, more tender, more silent. Now that he's less hungry for movement he savors Claudine-style, with the laziness of a gypsy, the grace of the present moment and despises what is better, but out of reach. He smiles more rarely, with a smile which remains and is slow to fade. Side by side, without speaking, we know how to look in front of us, free from impatience and curiosity, full of that slightly fearful melancholy which I call "the rustle of happiness."

Renaud, tired of women—but not of his wife—has renounced that collector's fever, that philatelist's anxiety which used to set him face to face with a new woman: "Ah, a specimen I hadn't got!" He loves more subtly, and from farther away. He fears the embarrassing gift and the tedious complication of permitted adultery, the chatter which causes the downfall of many a pretty creature . . . "Oh my silent darling! . . ." he says to me. And I know that he's remembering at that moment the sound of a never-ending voice which he would have liked to silence at its pink source with a handful of sand.

He tells fewer lies and gets angry more often. He vents his anger on some ornament or a fragile piece of furniture—a gesture for which he asks forgiveness later with a look. But I smile inwardly and say to myself: "That's me, that's me!"

Finally, my supreme victory! I've led him to love love in the way I do. I've made it chaste. Yes, chaste, and why not? He no longer introduces into what he used to call our "games" that *libertinage* that heeds the help of specially arranged mirrors, a book published in . . . Belgium, words made for whispering which are shouted out aloud and sound utterly crude.

He no longer needs this commonplace setup: He only needs me . . . and him. "Oh my silent darling!" he repeats again. Silent, yes, silent, except for the trembling sigh, the involuntary cry, the look and the gesture that are more expressive than a face. Oh, he must come back, the man I've modeled in my own likeness—he must come back and find himself face to face with one who no longer smiles, who turns away her attentive and confused eyes, at the moment when she abandons the whole of herself!

"My poor Annie . . ."
Fortunately she's neither mine nor poor; it's not my
pity that vents itself like this, but my remorse, a vague,
mean little scrap of remorse. I order her about or
forget her with the unkindness of a savage, the casual
behavior of an Indian, until I sense that beneath those
eyelids, as long and brown as almonds, her tears are
ready to come. She doesn't recognize me, neither do I.
Where are our idle days of the late autumn, and the
silent siestas against the warm wall, when we sat on
the ground, that friable soil protected by the tile
screen of the espalier, crumbling, white and pow-
dery, hardly ever damp! A bee, led astray by its
memory, would obstinately search above us for the

126

absent flowers on the apricot tree . . . Annie's hair was usually untidy, her carelessly braided pony tail hung down her back; and she would wait, with her eyes closed, until I chose to talk. . . .

The shadow of a man has changed all that. My base little female Annie, ingénue companion to men, who's kept her virginal face, has sided entirely with the one who wears the trousers. Misleading trousers, deceptive clothes, Annie! Are you hoping to change the face—if I may so describe it—of things? I know a freckled little wine grower at the bottom of the hill who would suit you much better—unless you've been close enough to Francis the gardener to be aware of his corn-colored moustache and his arms, smelling of fresh wood shavings and the stable?

In fact my stepson has spoiled everything here, ever since he's been trailing about like an idle prisoner, with his feeble, light step, and his vacant look, like aunt Anne—I mean sister Anne, who saw nothing coming.

No, he can't see anything coming, the little wretch! —and he'd rush off gaily by the first train. But I don't want to give him any money; I ought not to. And then I can't. It's a matter of a fairly big sum; I would have to tell my husband, tire him with explanations.

"We're snowed up," Renaud wrote to me, "we've ceased to inhabit the world of the living. O my darling, my faithful lamp, my belief must be strong for me to still see, through the whirling walls of this tomb, the anxious gleam of your sunstone-colored eyes . . . I'm going to come back, the snow can do nothing more for me. I'm going to come back just as I am, just as I see myself now, just as what I must admit to being: an old man. . . . The idea that I'm going to see you again makes me despair, even though it's what I live on. I know that your first glance will sum me up, that you'll assess my decline in one look; I know too that no sign of it will appear on your radiant little face, for your lies are faultless. For pity's sake, Claudine, don't lie to me, or I'll bury myself here. Shout, exclaim, raise your hands when you see me: 'Oh, my darling, how tired you are! how old you are! How white your hair is! Haven't you grown smaller? . . .' Reject everything that your pity would conceal, your pity that I don't want! Be honest without caution, overwhelm me, from the moment you first clasp your young arms around my scrawny old neck. Count my new wrinkles, smile at my old ones, run a tapering, condemnatory finger over creased eyelids; go to sleep all cold, full of disappointment and resentment; go to sleep sad and heavy-hearted, disenchanted with your old husband. . . . And perhaps the next day you'll find the poor man a little less ravaged when you compare him with your memory of the previous day . . ."

I shrugged my shoulders as I read the letter. I laughed with jerky laughter that made tears tremble in my eyes and rays of light dance between the letter and me. How silly he was to cover four pages with futile scribble, when three words would have been enough to fill the letter: "I'm coming back."

He's coming back. Two things matter now: the dress I'll wear the day he returns and the dinner menu for the same evening. For he'll come back in the evening, naturally. About the time when the sun sets at this season, half-past four, five o'clock. There'll be a blue dusk, the twilight will be mild and misty, or there'll be a hard frost, with two or three stars already visible above the sunset . . . the train gliding in, the smoke tasting of iodoform, the door, the plaid, the thick overcoat, the white moustache. . . . And then— I don't know—provided that it's not too cold and I haven't got a red nose. . . .

"Good news, Claudine?"

"Good news, Annie."

And I lowered my eyelids with a clumsily mysterious air while stroking Péronnelle, who was fast asleep on my lap. I shan't tell Annie anything tonight. Nor Marcel. I folded the envelope over my secret and put it into my pocket as though it were a biscuit that I'd eat in my room alone, at night. Nobody suspected that Renaud was coming back. Marcel was dozing on the edge of the divan, like Narcissus over the pool of water. Annie was embroidering, and heaven only knows what youthful memory, pink-skinned and muscular, crept in between herself and her canvas. Péronnelle was still asleep on her back, her breast exposed to all forms of torture. Her underbelly is pink and tawny, the color of a turtle dove, buttoned from top to bottom by four rows of black velvety marks. The regularity of her stripes allows her to retain, through the worst crises, the distinguished formal air of someone who is dressed by a good tailor. In her trusting sleep she revealed her naïve chin, the varnished outline of her curved mouth, and the four horn-tipped pads on her bohemian feet. She also didn't know that Renaud was coming back. . . .

A solitary little black creature, pug-nosed and silent, raised his odd muzzle up to me. That attractive little monster, Toby, awakened from his light sleep, was looking at me just as Matho looked at Salammbô. He didn't quite understand. He had had a premonition, he half-guessed, he was anxious and tried to come closer to me. Then I bent down to be near him, and with a pat on his bumpy head I told him that it was all right, that he had understood sufficiently, that there was nothing more to understand. . . .

What a pleasant evening! Now I've become once more what I should have been all the time; indulgent, relaxed, and optimistic. I turned toward "my poor Annie" with a look which asked forgiveness for my customary dryness, my angry silence of yesterday evening, but she was embroidering, her head was lowered, and my moist eyes fell on a pony tail which was tied with a black velvet bow. My all-embracing benevolence relished the abandoned grace of Marcel, who was sleeping as though he were in the theater, with one of his arms hanging down. A tongue of hissing blue gas leapt out of the crackling grate, announcing "news!" and the whole somnolent drawing room woke up.

"Are you doing poker work, Annie? I can hear the sound of the hot iron . . ." yawned Marcel.

Annie, her needle in the air, remained open-mouthed for a moment and her entire long delicate face revealed the shy look of a woman surprised in the midst of pleasure; it was so apparent that I hesitated for a moment between the desire to know whether she was dreaming and the desire to laugh at her.

"Annie! What are you thinking about? Quick, quick, no excuses, tell the truth!"

"I don't really know . . . vague things . . . I was sleepy, like Marcel. What's taken hold of you, Claudine?"

I leapt to my feet, to the great disgust of Péronnelle.

"Nothing! it's the effect of the frost. It's terribly hot in here. Suppose we open the windows a little." My two companions exchanged a look of horrified surprise.

"Open the windows!" cried Marcel. "She's crazy! We'd die! It's four degrees below freezing!"

Four degrees below freezing! How odd . . . odd and something of a shock. It's true; a humid, rustling night, a night full of jasmine and stars would have fulfilled me, extended my feeling—I who am overflowing with such selfish happiness this evening, I who can feel myself suddenly blossoming and exuding scent like a gardenia which has got the season wrong. . . . It's freezing . . . too bad.

"Leave that door alone, Claudine!" begged Marcel.

"Come here, I've had a blackhead on my forehead for two days. I haven't got the courage to squeeze it . . ."

"You mustn't squeeze it," said Annie hastily, "you must take a very fine needle and . . ."

She was interrupted by the squeaking of a mouse.

"A needle! Why not a scalpel? How ghastly, Annie! I'd rather put myself in the hands of Claudine. She squeezes my blackheads with an energy verging on sadism, and every time I feel I'm going to faint; I think she's torn open all my veins."

Marcel sat down on a foot rest shaped like a fishing boat, a little old-fashioned piece of furniture, pretentious and cumbersome. He held up his white face under the lamp, his eyes closed; he was already half-fainting, and Annie was so fascinated that she did not dare look away from the torture that was imminent.

Like a good-natured executioner I rested my two thumbnails against each other.

"Have you a handkerchief, Annie?"

"Yes, what for?"

"For the blood! I don't want any marks on my splendid shirtwaist, it cost twenty-nine francs. Where is this blackheaded ulcer? Yes, I can see it. My poor boy, you've called me in very late. The illness has made devastating inroads . . ."

Marcel's cheeks trembled between my hands with suppressed laughter and delectable anxiety. This delicate face with its closed eyes, transparent in the lamplight, lying in my hands like fruit . . . what other head have I held so carefully, whose head was so youthful and mysterious, whose face had such bloom, whose eyes were closed like this? Rézi . . . The comparison was strange—and unexpected. . . .

Annie bent over that closed, graceful face as over a mirror.

"Don't hurt him on purpose, Claudine," she murmured, feeling afraid.

"Don't be frightened, you little goose. He's too handsome for me to do him any damage, isn't he?"

"Oh, yes," she admitted softly, almost with respect. "It's funny, he's even better looking when his eyes are closed. It happens with very young men. The others look so anxious when they're asleep . . . you feel so far away from them. . ."

Marcel gave himself up to my hands, to our eyes. He enjoyed simultaneously our admiration, the caress of my warm hands and his childish terror of the hard pinch that he would soon feel on his temple. He didn't move, and breathed faintly and quickly with an imperceptible movement of his delicate nostrils. The shadow of his eyelashes brushed over his cheek like the shadow of a wasp's wing. Annie delighted in contemplating him; she had never had the intangible Marcel so near, so abandoned, so freely offered. She was comparing him with her most beautiful memories, and shook her head silently. . . . The longing for a kiss was so intense on her face that in spite of myself I searched Marcel's for the reflection of a desire so strong. . . .

A mouth which smiles because it's being desired, cheeks with a bloom of an intangible silver, youthful hair hanging down untidily over the forehead, fanning out silkily, eyes whose blue I know, hidden beneath eyelids more beautiful than a glance—there now, I'm holding it in my hand like a cup full to the brim; is this the young flesh from whom, according to Annie, some God should preserve me? Here is the unknown fruit whose taste they say surpasses all others. Here is the cause of Annie's downfall—and of many, many other women. This is what ruins and condemns so many old bacchantes who are ready to give up everything, but not this! "Young bodies!" These two words brush against my ear as though some thick-petaled flower had been held tightly and bruised. This is what I am holding in my hands, leaning over it with a calm and reasoning curiosity. . . . This is what can be found everywhere, given and sold, available to everyone . . . but not to me.

A little more curiosity, a little less love within me —and you'll become the prey, Claudine, of that all-devouring young flesh which perpetually torments my poor Annie! You'll give temporary names to your desperate suffering: Marcel, Paul—what's his name, Thingumabob—the page at the Palace, the schoolboy from the Lycée Stanislas. . . . You can despise Annie's intemperance because you aren't thirsty *yet* . . . But don't laughingly take a sip from her glass!

"Ow! Ooooo . . . you've never hurt me so much before! Is it bleeding?"

"Yes, but it's gone."

"You're sure? And the root as well?"

Marcel was awake now. He dabbed his temple and accepted from Annie's hands a little mirror "so that he could see the hole." I looked at him with a vaguely shrewd, slightly unkind expression, saying with a sigh of relief:

"Yes, it's all gone."

Two o'clock. The time for coffee, illustrated magazines, cigarettes of light tobacco with souls of blue smoke. It makes one feel indulgent and limp. When we left the dining room we'd opened the French windows just enough to shiver and say: "The fog's lifting—it'll freeze again tonight," just enough to see the fleeting shadow of the clouds rush by on vast chilly blue wings, just enough to feel envious as we scolded Péronnelle, who was sitting on the frozen steps and gazing serenely at the landscape, just as in summer, while the cold failed to contract the sensitive fur along her back. To look at her, it might have been August. We came back to the fire, to the table where the Saturday magazines, newly emerged from their cardboard tubes, were curling up like wood shavings. Their thick pages were black with photographs, and between them were cramped, winding pieces of text cut up into two lines here, three lines there, and further on four half lines which attempted, like hieroglyphics, to join up with their corresponding half above the picture of Madame Delarue-Mardrus—an article which deserved to be treated with greater respect. A diverting jumble of tenors, dogs, swimmers, duchess-poets, and titled motorists distracted my eyes, and I felt tired as I thought that so far away so many people were occupied in doing so many exhausting things.

"Do you find it very interesting, Annie, to learn that the Comtesse So-and-So's tortoise has just come third in a gymkhana? Are you thrilled to learn that the revival of *Tannhäuser*, with Rusinol, is (let's have a rare adjective!) brilliant?"

"Rusinol? Show me."

Annie came over, less slowly than usual, leaned over my shoulder and gazed vaguely for a long moment, her pale eyes glued to the portrait of the tenor with his bullfinch crop. Extended beyond her short profile I saw the soft flutter of her eyelashes, which possibly form her greatest beauty, so long, so dark, their delicate tips slightly tinged with auburn. She owes to them almost the entire charm of her face, and their fanlike fluttering endows her with that expression of false decorum and guilty emotion which makes people want to disturb her even more.

"Rusinol . . ." she murmured finally. "How he's changed!"

"Do you know him?"

She shook her head, and her queue, plaited like the tail of a cart horse, flopped from one shoulder to the other:

"Not really! I—how do you put it—I was . . . with him a little during the year when he won that first prize."

"Did you . . . go to bed together?"

"Bed . . . that's an overstatement. There wasn't even a chaise-longue in his place: only a table, little chairs, and a high-backed armchair."

"And no bed?"

"Oh, the bed! Anything was better than the bed, Claudine! The armchair seemed the most comfortable place. So I think it would be more accurate to say that Rusinol and I, we . . . we sat down together . . ."

She smiled with natural kindheartedness. She looked as though she were describing her first ball dress while I, feeling slightly embarrassed, was leafing through a copy of *Fémina*—which smelled of glue—to give myself countenance.

"It sounds like some naughty novel. Did those acrobatics amuse you?"

She hesitated:

"They amuse me . . . now! I think I was silly, I have to laugh at myself. But at that moment . . . no, Claudine, it's not a happy memory. I'm quite ready to tell you about it because I tell you everything . . ."

"Oh, everything . . ."

"Yes, yes!" protested Annie. "You must understand me! When I begin a story about—"

"—a travel story—"

"Thank you . . . I tell you the *whole* story, I don't try to make excuses for myself or disguise the man of the moment as Prince Charming. If I describe what happened, without any intention of boasting or deceiving you, isn't that 'telling everything?' "

She laughed, showing her small teeth; their hard enamel looked slightly blue between lips whose redness was tinged with purple like the inside of a half-eaten cherry. Annie rarely laughs openly, and whenever she does her laughter is disconcerting, revealing sharp teeth and a strong moist interior to her mouth, while her face is small and anemic-looking. Whenever I saw her laugh as I saw her at that moment I would say to myself: "What idiots we all are! Her husband, her sister-in-law Marthe, and I myself, none of us could see that within Annie there existed a demanding, totally mature creature, hungry for young flesh, a strong animal that sooner or later would run away . . ." I would sigh, resigned, as Maugis says, to letting myself be taken in once more.

"Come on then, Annie, tell me . . . everything."

"Everything . . . that won't take long, Claudine. You see Rusinol as he is now, with his fat little tummy, he's already getting a double chin, and he has a nose like a Roman emperor. That photograph nauseates me! How ridiculous he looks in a Romeo part! And that hand on the scabbard of the sword! And those rings! Within a year he's going to be utterly ridiculous. Oh, I know . . ." She recovered herself, slightly embarrassed by her spiteful words. "I know perfectly well that his eyes are still very fine, even allowing for makeup and retouching . . . but that picture can't possibly show you what Rusinol used to be like—he was called simply Louis Rusinol in those days—the year he won the first prize, four years ago —no, three . . . no, four in fact . . . anyway, that doesn't matter. A little firebrand from the south, he was quite wiry, quite dark, as lively as a *pelota* player, he had a hard, olive-skinned face, and all you could see of it at first was an angry quivering nose and a pair of eyes that would scorch anything in sight. He would say to anyone ready to listen that he'd 'eat everyone up,' that he'd 'outdo the lot of them,' all the tenors of France and Italy, and that low-class, dreary breed of German tenors. You had neither eyes nor ears for anyone else; he expressed himself in every possible way. In the street or in a courtyard, anywhere, he would pour out brilliant high C's which would bounce back from the walls like brass bullets.

141

At the same time he was flirtatious, and spiteful, and proud; if he heard any other singer being praised his nostrils would go quite white! You might find him unbearable but you didn't forget him. I'd met him through Auguste . . ."

"Auguste . . . now which one was that?"

"The mime-drama man—the one you called Lord Vendramin. . ."

"Oh yes, of course . . . thank you. Go on!"

"They'd been fellow students at the Conservatoire; Auguste, Rusinol, and I had sometimes lunched together at Drouant's . . . Rusinol amused me, he left me gasping: I used to watch him talk, sing, and move with the same nervous astonishment you feel when you watch people juggling with knives. So, when Lord Vendramin went off to America with Sarah's company, it wasn't very difficult for Rusinol to . . . I don't know how it happened . . ."

"While listening to that nightingale singing . . ."

"More or less. It was a day when he'd found me all alone at Drouant's, eating eggs with tomatoes, which I hate, and weeping vaguely into the food. Auguste had left the day before, with hardly a farewell kiss. I thought it was very nice of Rusinol to console me, to run down Auguste and take my hands in his: 'We artists, my dear, we mustn't abandon ourselves to common sorrows. We leave each other, we come together again, it's all utterly stupid. The only thing is work, it comes first, it keeps you going.

You'll never do anything in the theater if you behave like a doormat. You need a gay, lively companion who can raise your morale and galvanize you into action; he must even be able to find you a little engagement if necessary . . ." And at the same time he was doing a very difficult trick with Swedish matches, which didn't stop him from looking right into my eyes in such a way that if I'd been standing I'd have collapsed into a chair. . . . I'd got such a headache, a terrible headache! And at the same time I wanted to cry, and sleep, and laugh too, for he took me for a little theatrical tart—so much so that after lunch he called the waiter with such a splendid B flat that the windows rattled, and he took my arm. A quarter of an hour later, well . . ."

I sat up, startled. "What do you mean? A quarter of an hour later!"

"He lived in the rue Gaillon," she explained simply. "The time it took to go up five flights of stairs, throw his hat on the bed and me into the armchair . . . sparrows in the gutter go about it the same way. I tell you: a quarter of an hour later I became his mistress, and I was weeping from nerves and tiredness and lack of satisfaction, and also because he'd been so quick and rather rough. And as I sought for at least his shoulder where I could hide and relax a little, and his mouth which was also hard, active, and almost cruel . . . what did I hear? I heard chords being banged out while he sang *vocalises* to 'A-a-a

143

a-a-a' Rusinol was sitting at the piano in his under-pants, but he had kept his jacket on and was vocaliz-ing, carefully, *mezza voce,* then higher and higher, 'A-a-a-a-a . . .' up to his famous high C, keen and glittering as the blade of a lance . . . I couldn't believe it! Suddenly he turned around, leapt at me and began all over again! And he went just as fast, like an im-perious little cockerel thinking only of his own plea-sure—the same letdown for me, unfortunately—and immediately afterwards, the same cascade of *vocalises* (that was more or less the only . . . waterfall I experi-enced with him!) and then we began all over again. He spent his time doing that, pulling up a woman's skirts, having her in five minutes, and quick, quick, off to the piano to make sure it hadn't damaged his high C! Oh, you can imagine the disillusionment I suffered! That damnable Rusinol, those eyes which seemed to burn everything up—he would burn on his own, like that dry hemp seed you use to light the fire here in winter. There was never time to catch up with him!"

"Never?"

"Never!"

"And yet you went back again, didn't you?"

"Yes," she admitted, humble and truthful. "His love-making was painful, upsetting and futile, like grief that's interrupted too soon, like a punishment that isn't fully received. I nearly always cried after-wards. . . ."

"Didn't that worry him?"

"Him? No. He sang his beautiful C and then he would tap me on the shoulder, bestowing on me a look that was never surprised: 'Poo-er little thing . . . she's grateful . . .'"

$\mathcal{A}$ soft rustling against the closed shutters, a monotonous but expressive whisper, close to speech, woke me gradually. . . . I recognized the silken murmur of snow. Snow already! It must be falling in heavy flakes, from a calm sky undisturbed by the wind . . . falling vertically and slowly. It's darkening the early morning and choking the children on their way to school; they're meeting it with their noses up in the air and their mouths open, as I used to do in the past. . . .

And ironically the night had filled me with sunny, childlike dreams, facile, empty dreams containing only my childhood, summer, warmth, and thirst. . . .

It must be a slight temperature that's still keeping

me in the summertime and the garden that belonged to my childhood. I'm thirsty. But I'm thirsty only for water, colored with the everyday dark red wine that Mélie used to pour out for me in the cool, slightly musty dining room. . . . "I want a drink, Mélie, quickly!"

She would bang the door, a low grating would squeak, and up the dark steps would come the smell of seed potatoes germinating in the cellar, the smell of sour wine spilt on the sandy floor of the wine compartment, a scent so damp and icy cold that a quiver of delight would run down between my shoulders, which were sweaty from dashing about or playing skittles. Yes, I'm thirsty only for wine that has no bouquet, drunk only from the kitchen tumbler that felt thick against my lips, and where my experienced tongue could feel a bubble blown into the coarse glass.

"Another glass, Mélie!"

"No, I tell you. You'll get frogs in your tummy."

The usual remark which I heard each time with an almost enjoyable irritation, like all Mélie's other sayings . . . "When a dog finds a little girl's tooth on the ground and swallows it, the little girl grows a dog's tooth and the dog grows a little girl's tooth . . ." "Don't put your playmates' hats on during break: Sweat from three different people makes you go bald!"

Dazed by the sudden darkness, I would guess where to find on the table the four-o'clock bread, the loaf that was still warm, and I broke open the fragrant crust, took out the soft part and poured raspberry jelly on it . . . *goûter*, the afternoon snack! my favorite meal when I was a schoolgirl, the varied emergency store that I could carry off to the main branch of the walnut tree, or into the barn, or to evening playtime, a hectic time when we managed to eat while running about, laughing or playing hopscotch, without anyone choking to death. . . .

Then I would go back to the golden, humming garden, with its sickly sweet smell of wistaria and honeysuckle, the enchanted wood hung with green pears, red and white cherries, downy apricots and hairy gooseberries.

Oh, June of my dreams! Early summer when everything is swollen with acid juice! Crushed grass which marked my white dress and my snuff-colored stockings, cherries I would prick with a pin, their pale pink blood quivering in round drops. . . . Gooseberries, green beneath the tongue, that I would crush open with timid teeth, gooseberries that one suspects of being horrible and are always worse!

I want only reddened water, drunk in the dark dining room of my childhood, from the glass which is thick against my lips. . . .

It's snowing. I'm waiting for Renaud. Marcel's bored. Annie embroiders, remembers and hopes. Yesterday I left the two of them:

"Annie, don't get Marcel pregnant!"

And off I went across the newly fallen snow, my legs encased in woolen gaiters!

O lovely immaculate garden! The only marks on it are the blue of the fir trees, a rusty clump of chrysanthemums, and the mauve crop of a hungry wood pigeon. . . .

Péronnelle is intoxicated; yellow, gray, tawny, striped and spotted, her eyes glowing like lanterns, she changes into a panther in the hope of gorging herself on unwary sparrows—but her color gives her away, even when she lies flat in the snow, her ears back, her eyebrows touching and her tail swaying. She can never have regretted so much that she's not a chameleon: "Oh, I *would* like to be white!" her beautiful fierce eyes beseech me. . . . Toby, black and polished, follows on my heels sneezing, and I'd swear that he's trying to print a naïve drawing of four little hollow flowers between my long footprints. You're clinging to me like a squat shadow, little dog with the gift of divination, you who know that I won't leave you, as Annie would, to run over to a little beribboned page boy, all green and gold, with cheeks like apples. . . .

The air leaves us breathless, air heavy with waiting snow, without a hint of wind. I call Toby, and my voice doesn't travel far, as though I were in a room muffled with hangings. Everything is so changed that I walk along with the delightful certainty of losing my way. The smell of the snow, that delicate scent of water, ether and dust, obscures all other smells. The little bull terrier, anxious because he can no longer feel the way, questions me frequently. I reassure him and we go down the road where a double row of wheelmarks can hardly be seen, along with green egg-shaped droppings surrounded by a flight of tits. . . . "So, on, Toby, into the woods!"

"So far!" Toby answers with his eyes. "Aren't you afraid of that strange forest kingdom with all the snow, where the daylight filters sadly through, as in a church? And how silent it is! Heavens! Something moved..."

"No, no, Toby, it was a yellow leaf falling slowly, straight down, like a tear..."

"A leaf ... it was a leaf when you looked at it, but ... before you looked at it, who can say what it was? It came near, like a light step, and then like someone drawing breath.... Come on! I'm afraid. I can't see the sky over our heads anymore, for the tops of the fir trees are joined together. A short time ago I was looking at a buried world, but beneath this undulating mantle I could see the outlines of familiar shapes: the rounded humpbacked mountain opposite our house and four naked poplar trees which I use as landmarks. Come on! Something cried out quite near..."

"But, Toby, it was the big brown jay that's flying away over there, with the blue edge to his wings..."

"A jay?... yes. Just now it's a jay, but just before, when it cried out, what was it? You know only one aspect of things and creatures, the one you see. I know two: the one I see and the one I don't see, which is more frightening..."

This is how we converse, for Toby, full of fear and faith, finds in my eyes an inexhaustible supply of the courage he needs to go fifteen yards farther on, then he has to stop, look at me and start off again....

The faith that animals have in us, overwhelming and undeserved faith! Sometimes animals give us looks which make us turn away; we blush, we try to defend ourselves: "No, no! I haven't deserved this devotion, this gift without regret or reserve; I haven't done enough, I feel unworthy . . ."

As light as an elf, a little squirrel flies along in front of us from branch to branch. Its russet tail fans out like smoke, its fleecy front moving up and down as he leaps along. He's plumper, better upholstered and richer than an angora rabbit and leans down to look at me, his forelegs wide apart, his fingernails holding on in human fashion. His beautiful black eyes quiver with a timid effrontery, and I yearn to catch hold of him, to feel his tiny little body beneath the soft fleece; it's so pleasurable to imagine that it makes me clench my teeth slightly.

All at once it's almost dark. Because the ground's white one forgets that night can fall, and one only thinks of it when it's there. The little bull terrier trembles at my feet while I stand upright and with my tired eyes search for the way as we come out of the dark woods. Nothing stirs beneath the shuttered sky, and the dark bird that flies away from me seems to remain silent on purpose . . . I hesitate, for I'm lost, deprived of the red glow which should be tingeing the west and guiding me toward home. It's a very minor, fabricated anxiety but one which I cherish and exaggerate with the enjoyment of a childish Robinson Crusoe. The sky comes down toward the snow, now turning blue, it weighs down on me, it will crush me; I'm a poor creature without a shell, without a house. . . . Come now, a little more imagination, a little more anxiety still, you waking dreamer! Say to yourself again, almost aloud, words which at this moment have a mysterious power: "Night . . . snow . . . solitude . . ." Let a frightened and primitive soul escape from yours! Forget mankind and the road, and the friendly house, forget everything except the darkness, fear, hunger which harries you and reduces your courage; listen, your ears trembling and shaking beneath your hair; watch, your eyes enlarged and blind, for the footstep that follows you as you run, the shape darker than the night which could rear up here, there, in front, behind. . . . Flee, happy in your fear, you don't believe in it! Flee and feel your heart in your mouth, hear Toby's breathless choking. Flee faster, pursued by the shadow of shadow, glide over the snow which is freezing and cracks open like a broken window; flee as far as the heaven which your instinct finds again, as far as the red-glowing door against which you stumble, trembling like the squirrel, where you sigh, your intoxication over: "Already!"

We're kept indoors by ghastly rain and move irritably between the fire, which is too hot, and the French windows, where the east wind whistles. There's nothing we can do about it. The moment I half-open one side of the window a deafening sound of lapping water can be heard, riddling the stone steps, and endless drops ricochet onto the polished wooden floor. When I raise the curtain, we can see behind it the rain moving along, a transparent, funereal curtain which slowly drags its irregular folds toward the west, like the skirts of some giantess crossing the rounded sides of the mountains one by one.

The fire and the waiting make me impatient, for

I'm counting the days and the nights. I keep silent. "I dig into myself," as I used to say in the past . . . I wear myself out conscientiously, with a patient impatience that's already received its reward, for I can see one hour that shines out among all the others. . . .

Annie and Marcel make me unhappy. They look like prisoners in solitary confinement, torn by nervous yawns and shivering. In vain has Marcel changed his tie three times and, just before dinner, despairingly swapped his hunting boots (?) for a pair of patent leather pumps. . . . He wanders about, languishing from a constraint which only I, after Renaud, can bring to an end. What a blue gleam would come into his girlish eyes, what a smooth color to his velvety cheek if I suddenly said to him: "Look, here are your hundred and fifty louis, you can go now . . ." I'll take good care not to give him that pleasure. In the first place, three thousand francs—I'd have to ask Renaud for that amount, and what excuse could I give? And then—I have to admit it on this tempting sheet of blank paper—I secretly enjoy my stepson's childish boredom. It's the despicable instinct of a captive! Wanting to move one's impatience about without curing it, disguising it with laughter, serenity or indifference, what have I been doing for so many weeks? Yes, I like watching Annie savor her suffering in a silence of sexual yearning, and Marcel, pale with solitude, savoring, even in front of Annie, anecdotes in which petticoats have no place at all. I offer them my own grief like a *gâteau* sprinkled with sand. . . .

How unkind I am! We won't worry, it will pass. It's a wet evening. The sunshine will come back with *him,* it will be silvery too and snowy, all sweetened with hoarfrost. Annie will be able to escape then—what strong young body will she seek?—and Marcel, toward what dubious lad? And everything will become easy again, light, durable, natural. We haven't got long to wait now. Let's stay here, children, in our soaking wet ark which this deluge seems to have hoisted to the top of the mountain. Be patient, do as I do, travel with your feet upon a cushion, your hands clasped beneath your chin. Marcel's picking out on the piano the liquid, childlike song of the Rhine maidens taunting Siegfried, and now I'm almost ten years younger; I'm back in that year 19—, the beginning and end of one of Renaud's swift and sudden flirtations, which burn briefly with a disturbing glare, but leave only a handful of ashes behind, white and drifting like down. . . .

That year Renaud was in love with the beautiful Suzie. The beautiful Suzie was attractive through an Americanism within reach of the most mediocre French novelists. She had long, slender legs and a fairly natural waist; her shoulders resembled those of a Prussian officer, and her small head was built on simple, straightforward lines: a wide jaw line and an unsatisfactory nose saved by the feline curve of her nostrils. Suzie laughed too often, but she revealed moist teeth, their edges uneven like the second teeth of ten-year-old children. Whenever she laughed she closed her eyes and you thought only of her mouth, the one feature that still shone in her face. But when her dark brown eyes opened again you followed in fascinated exhaustion their anxious, defiant and tender restlessness.

Her clothes and hair styles were chaotic, ranging from the "Rat-Mort" boater to the most flowery extravagance. For her ancestors, the Red Indians, had bequeathed to her an ingrained taste for wearing a feather behind her ear, in the absence of a ring through her nose. Her feet were graceful but her hands boyish, and her voice, which could whisper and drawl with ambiguous sweetness, became nasal and hard as soon as it was raised.

Literature had spoiled this fine Yankee bird, who should have been taught only to shine, move her head up and down beneath feathers blown about by the wind, to show her teeth, the redness beyond her lips, and kick away the downy trains that she tossed about and fastened up like a real Negress in all her finery. . . .

Suzie had read, and that was the cause of all the trouble. She had read a good deal and remembered little; she'd mixed a bilingual salad of poetry and prose, drama, novels, and philosophy into which she dipped at random, choosing none too carefully, with a confidence that produced naïve admiration.

I didn't feel bitter when Renaud began to follow Suzie from five o'clock rendezvous to afternoon tea parties. She was so little like me! I'm sure I'd fill the world with shouting and bloodshed if my husband fell in love with a woman as silent as me but violent beneath it all, her violence softened with laziness, contemplative and active like me, and prettier and younger.

But Suzie! What Claudine could have been jealous of Suzie? Suzie avid for flirting and risky caresses underneath the tablecloth. Suzie, absorbing and given to lying, Suzie whose date book was fuller than a dentist's, Suzie who was willingly utilitarian, knowing how to borrow from this or that painter or novelist a so-called "original" opinion which she took over in a self-important way, like a little girl parading about in a skirt that's too long. . . .

For this beautiful Suzie, Renaud once more expended his proselyte's enthusiasm, in spite of my sage advice. "She's beautiful," I would repeat to him, "what more do you want her to be? Teach her how to remain silent, she'll come closer to perfection . . ." And then I would laugh when I heard my husband plead Suzie's cause against me, find that she had finesse, a totally Latin promptness of mind, even an honorable melancholy and a basic dislike of snobbery

. . . Suzie melancholy! Melancholy and full of a noble desire for better things, that trooper's mare, snorting proudly beneath the pompoms and plumes!

(In spite of myself I'm disparaging her a little too much. A belated jealousy takes hold of me as I remember so many lost hours, days wasted in meetings here and there which deprived me of Renaud.)

My dear husband's loving apostolate ended in the strange project of taking Suzie to Bayreuth with us, during the summer of that same year, 19—. I almost wept; then I foresaw, sensibly, the normal end to this idyll, and realized that Suzie herself would kill Suzie. . . .

For the second time I saw without pleasure the grubby little town with its rain of soot, the margrave's garden where Annie, dazed with solitude, had collapsed on my shoulder. I saw again on my plate horrible things *mit Kompott* and in my glass the mediocre but chilled beer. I saw again the preposterous beds, enemies of sleep and love-making, the fragmented beds, their sheets too short, the mosaic-type mattresses in three sections, the coffinlike beds covered during the day by a planklike lid of printed cretonne . . . O Franconian beds! I've tried you all ways; you force people to turn pleasure into acrobatics!

Renaud had chosen for Suzie a cheerful little old-fashioned apartment whose windows, decked with pink pelargoniums sweetened with dust, opened onto the Richard Wagnerstrasse, which was burning hot and deserted. When I say deserted!—twice a day a Bavarian regiment marched down it, strong young men in uniforms of dirty gray, riding large chestnut nags, their likeable sun-baked, bulldog faces showing between their helmets and their raspberry-colored woolen collars. . . .

I saw again, like a snapshot where each detail shone brilliantly, those two flower-decked windows and Suzie's head and shoulders as she leaned against the rail. She was bareheaded, and her brown hair, twisted into the shape of a shell, shone with gold highlights in the noonday sun; her breasts were slightly crushed against her arms, and she wore a loose dress with a painted design of pink and yellow fir cones; her little nose wrinkled as she tried to keep her eyes open against the blazing sun. Close behind her Renaud's tall figure formed a bar of shadow, cutting across the white background of the room. She laughed, and leaned farther out over the sound of the passing regiment, over the cloud of dust which rose up toward her, over the smell of leather, horses, and men in wet clothes. She laughed and the steaming soldiers responded to her laughter, their faces raised and their teeth bared. She crushed her breasts against her arms, tilted her dovelike neck backward and murmured: "All those men . . . it's funny, so many men at once . . ." Her fine coffee-colored look met that of my husband, then moved quickly away, and we all three remained serious and silent, like three strangers brought together by chance. Yes, I remember that decisive moment! I distinctly saw, between Suzie and Renaud, the flight of their desire, which stopped for a second, its wings extended, and flew away in fright like those sparrows which suddenly utter shrill cries after feeling the shadow of an evil bird pass over them. . . . However, I had masked my expression, contained the murderous thoughts that I kept hidden in the depths of myself, quivering and well-disciplined like a good hunting dog that awaits a sign. . . . I didn't make the sign. . . . What would have been the use? The one I love must live freely, in a soothing, illusory liberty. . . .

Each day that followed that anxious moment Renaud was able to see and cherish his Suzie, to accept the caress of her singsong accent, her floating feathers, her changing scent—a mixture which she varied in haphazard fashion and which suited her, whether it was sweet or sharp—and be present, in her untidy bedroom, at the last intoxicating moments of her toilet. . . .

At noon I would heroically send him to collect Suzie among the scattered lingerie, the untidy basins, the half-empty trunks. I knew that she greeted both him and the flowers he brought every day with a half embarrassed, half-cheerful "Oh," and then she fastened the waistband of her skirt with skillful clumsiness. . . . I could imagine her, leaning toward the mirror but looking elsewhere, sharpening her mouth with two strokes of "grape," shaking her powder puff and adding velvety down to her cheeks, never looking at herself, with the skill of a female monkey who knew how to apply makeup. I knew so well—better than Renaud—the false hatred, the false untidiness, the false perplexity of Suzie, whose dark eyes became darker and troubled with such a pulsating anxiety that one thought in spite of oneself about the guilty motive behind such strong feelings. . . .

In fact, I'd been able to see all that through the walls, before Renaud allowed himself to tell me everything. . . . Poor dear man, he finally fell into the trap of my confidence and serenity, and I really believe, from the pain that I endured from the moment of his first confidence, that I didn't ask for so much. . . .

Heroic—I was heroic; the word is not too strong! I underwent, as passive as any foreign governess, the "tetralogy lessons" in which Renaud sublimated his passion while Suzie assimilated them in silent ecstasy, her eyes fixed on those of the benevolent apostle with the silvery moustache. Didn't I almost scratch her face one day when I noticed that she wasn't listening to Renaud's voice?—she was following instead, her eyes full of blackness, the movement of his lips.

Let's forget all that, let's forget it! Let us remember only my silent delight, the sudden urge to "dance the jig" which took hold of me one evening, one splendid evening, the evening of *Parsifal*. . . .

In the Theatre Restaurant, that uncomfortable hall which smelled of sauce, spilled beer, and bad cigars, we were waiting, in utter exhaustion, for a tepid wiener schnitzel to come to our table, borne on the tide of an audience left frantic with hunger after a four-hour performance. Seated under a dismal overhead light with my elbows on the table, I was watching Renaud, aged by the music, his moustache quivering, his jaws set hard; Suzie was rejuvenated and lively, the crushing harmony had mercifully glided over her head. She was pretending to be tired, twisting her supple shoulders, lowering her eyelids, swaying backward and forward in a voluptuous gymnastic performance which Renaud relished in a silent, almost ill-intentioned way. Around us was a din of plates, exclamations, orders called out in bad German by Maugis, who was sitting at a table behind us with the Payet couple and Annie, the cries of a gaggle of Englishwomen without hats . . . they sounded like guinea fowl. As for me, I was thinking guiltily that at ten o'clock a train would be leaving for Carlsbad and that the Carlsbad express would carry Claudine off to Paris, a Claudine who was tired of everything and more or less neglected. . . .

"Oh yes," affirmed Suzie, with an assumed and highly attractive fervor, "I cried my eyes out during the baptism scene!"

And she opened her eyes wide; they had the shimmering brown color of the Seine at night.

"Yes . . ." murmured Renaud, barely in control of himself.

"Oh, I recognized it clearly, the Spear motif!"

"The Spear motif! What Spear motif?"

I leaned forward attentively, suddenly illuminated with hope. . . .

"But Renaud, the Spear motif, the one that's used for Wotan, and for Parsifal too, well, I'm not wrong, am I?"

From my brief smile the beautiful Suzie sensed her mistake, but Maugis, who was practically drunk, indiscreetly applauded her from where he sat:

"Yessir, pretty lady, yessir! And your leitmotif teacher ought to be devilish proud of you, if I may say so. The Spear motif! The one that's used for Wotan, for Siegfried's sword, for Parsifal's rapier, for Hans Sachs's awl, for Hunding's hunting knife and for Senta's nail file! Three cheers for the Spear motif, collective, collapsible and interchangeable! It'll make Wollzogen and Chamberlain into two slices of fried potato—*mit kompott!*"

Fat, sweating, puffing Maugis, I could have kissed him! Suzie blushed, and was prettier for being cross; Renaud decided to utter an indulgent, paternal laugh, but he turned his eyes away from mine so that I couldn't see the hint of angry irritation in them. As for me, I felt a vindictive delight take hold of me, run along my veins and tickle my skin from beneath; I allowed my thoughts to abandon the train to Carlsbad, and as I tipped back my head to drain my emerald green römer, filled with a Johannisberg wine as dry and clear-cut as a blow, I murmured: "Be charming and don't talk . . ."

And I began to get tipsy on purpose, in order to celebrate the glorious brick that had been dropped; I drank to Maugis, who returned the compliment freely; I drank to Annie, who was pale and prostrated; she smiled at me without understanding, with the absentminded look of a schoolgirl who's got bad habits . . . I drank to Marthe Payet and her husband; he was reserved as usual, she was striking and redheaded, her hair dressed in broad waves beneath an aggressive hat—she looked like a Helleu copied by Fournéry . . . I drank, already feeling intoxicated, to my dear Renaud, raising my glass to him for a silent wish. And Suzie, amused and unresentful, filled my römer once more, laughing heartily, her eyes shut and her teeth exposed, to make me drink to the health of her absent husband, that husband who was toiling for her in distant Russian oil fields.

I gazed at my double image in my own drunkenness, I saw my flushed cheeks, my red mouth, my curls softening in the heat, and I felt the pupils of my eyes were so dilated and yellow that their light was heating my eyelids. I talked and talked, taking advantage of my physical felicity and my temporary duality to express all the facile jokes which I keep to myself out of laziness and modesty when I'm sober. I remember that at the height of my chatter I could see the faces of Renaud, Suzie, Annie, Marthe, and Léon, plus that of Maugis, congested and masklike, turned toward me, attentive and bantering—they looked at me with the expression of people watching without being seen, or observing a blind woman without fear of discovery. A blind woman! My warm eyes entered into their souls, with curiosity but not without scorn, and only felt cooler and disarmed when they encountered the blue-black water of Renaud's eyes, a Renaud who was undecided, shaken, and wondering about the secret motives behind this unrestrained intoxication. . . .

As from that day I no longer counted my victories. O you, all you Suzies, if only you knew what's involved when love for a man, as you call it, is really: desire! . . .

A moment came when I discerned, in Renaud's edgy behavior, something that wasn't desire: the urge, discreet at first, frantic and abnormal later, to be off. Had Suzie yielded to him? I never knew. I don't want to know. Renaud told me only too much about it, afterwards. I learned through him what crude and "female" snares she used, with what undignified, almost professional physical contacts she teased him, and how she would rub her scented head against him, murmuring: "I'm a poor little woman all on my own, I do so need to be petted . . ." I learned how Suzie would open her husband's letters in front of Renaud and read them with a knowing, rapid glance, without skipping a line, and on her face that canine smile which bared her teeth. . . . One day she was more wicked than usual and thrust a crumpled letter in front of Renaud: "Read that if it amuses you. . . . Yes, yes, read it!" And her supple, perpetually cold hands smoothed out the letter, four pages covered with thick, clear handwriting. Renaud read, with Suzie leaning on his shoulder. He read, suddenly frozen like Suzie's hands, the most humble, the most heartbreaking letter that an absent husband, disillusioned and jealous, can write to a woman he's idiotically in love with: "My own Suzie, my love . . . you're so far away . . . be good, but do everything that you like doing. Take care of yourself. . . . Don't be unfaithful to me, my love. . . . You know how sad I am and how unhappy you can make me—don't be unfaithful to me, you're all I have in the world . . ."

That repeated, humiliated and hopeless cry: *don't be unfaithful to me*, the servility of that man who accepted everything in order to keep Suzie, and the insulting gaiety of that bitch leaning over the letter, her cheek touching Renaud's moustache. .... All that scene which brought the Franconian idyll to an end was something I didn't see, but I sketched it in my memory and I handle it lovingly, like a devotional picture, like a fetish that has proved its worth. . . .

"Annie, if the weather's going to cloud over like this, perhaps Polisson ought to be given winter shoes? One of his forelegs isn't too good as it is, and if it freezes he won't be able to bring Renaud back from the station on Tuesday, will he?"

Annie sat there, her hands idle, with that vacant, disused air which I find either upsetting or infuriating. I thought she wasn't showing enough excitement. Renaud was coming on Tuesday, after all! I wanted to shout the words out to her, drive them hard into that head with its narrow temples. . . .

"Well, Annie?"

She shrugged her shoulders and enveloped me in

her vague blue gaze. "*I* don't know. Why should I care if Polisson has winter shoes or not? For weeks now you've relieved me of thinking about my house, my farmer, the menus for meals. I've given you everything with Casamène, the house, the grounds, the worries of being a property owner—everything. Keep them."

"You're right, Annie . . ."

And I was suddenly surprised by my conciliatory meekness! The master was approaching. He was arriving, and already I had bowed my head to accept the collar that was too loose, the illusory shackle from which I could escape without even unfastening it, if I wanted to. But I didn't want to. I'd said, "You're right." I'll also say: "As you wish, Renaud. . . . Please . . . yes . . . allow me . . ." It was time for words of deference and affection to come back into my vocabulary and replace the imperatives with which I'd been castigating the limp Annie and the shifty Marcel. . . .

The latter was lurking about just behind us, ill from idleness and anxious about his father's return. He was avoiding the bitter east wind; last week it had peeled off the delicate skin from the rims of his ears.

"Now, Marcel, go and put these coat hangers up in the big wardrobe for me. I'm making some room here for Renaud's clothes."

He obeyed, his hands unwilling and his expression pleasant, apparently afraid of breaking one of his nails. My room—soon to be our room—was strewn with linen and dresses. I was tidying up, drunk with untidiness; my belt was twisted, my cravat hanging down, a lock of hair in the shape of a question mark hid first one cheek, then the other. From time to time the faint worry that I might be looking hideous interrupted me and I dashed to the triple mirror to ask an opinion . . . ugh! . . . it would be all right . . . it was all right. The firmness of my figure concealed my true age . . . the yellow color of my eyes offset the new hollowness of my cheeks and my "bracketlike" lip seemed surprised at remaining so childlike. *He* would forget, once again, to notice, between these horizontal eyes and this curving mouth, the dry sharpness of the chin and jaws, the inadequacy of the cheeks that were losing their down, the wrinkles sketched in like more brackets at the corners of my mouth, and the strange mauve arrow-shaped shadow, which emphasized the inner angle of my eyelids. . . . Don't worry, don't worry, it'll be all right. . . .

"Take those over there, Annie, they're summer blouses."

"Where, over there?"

"The big wardrobe in the darkroom, where Marcel's hanging up coat hangers. It's dark there, stretch your hands out in front of you. If you hear something, call out; it'll be Marcel."

"Oh," she cried, modestly, but she hurried off; you never could tell. . . .

I went on tidying up. Out of a cardboard box, badly tied and bursting open at all corners, fell yellow papers, badly developed little photographs, rolled up in tubes and turning brown. With difficulty I could pick out the highlights of a splendid self-indulgent trip that Renaud and I made to Belle-Île-en-Mer, eight years ago now. . . .

Sarah Bernhardt had not yet brought civilization to the Pointe des Poulains nor leveled its light sand which flows rapidly through your fingers in a cold dry stream, scintillating with thousands upon thousands of crushed rubies, sequined with every shade of pink and mauve.

Earthbound creature that I was, astonished and won over by the sea, I have never enjoyed it so much as I did there. A salty fever made my heart beat faster at night and electrified my sleep, while during the day the sea air intoxicated me until I was dead tired and gave in to sleep in the hollow of a rock or on the striped sand which powdered my hair. The ocean licked my brown spindly shanks and polished my toenails—I always went barefoot. I was never tired of watching the fishing boats set out over the sharp, hard blue-green of the waves, boats with sails sloping like wings of coral pink or faint turquoise, making the color of the waves more brilliant and more unreal.

An eager laziness shortened the hours. Like two cheerful dogs going out scavenging together, we occupied ourselves with a threatening cloud or a change in the wind, and I haven't forgotten Renaud with bare legs and arms, his finger gravely extended toward a furious crab who was crazy with bravado, jumping and clicking his claws. He was quite red, as though he'd been already boiled. Seaside rain, the fine, vapor-like rain that powders your cheek and hair with a silvery mist, soaked us on one side while the wind dried us on the other. Only hunger sent us back to our big wooden house which smelled like a ship, and I would quickly climb the steps, passionately keen to sniff the court bouillon of baby lobsters or the stew of sliced tuna fish, as solid as veal. I would bound up the steps, leaving behind me the marks of my bare feet, as cool and damp as the feet of a savage. . . .

In the evening a plaintive, gentle humming sound would draw us out onto the pink brick balcony. By the light of the stars the Bigouden sardine workers, their arms linked, were moving in a circle and singing, while their close-knit farandole was danced to a jerky, strange rhythm of five beats to a bar:

> No, no, no, the man I love
> He baint here at all. . . .

By the light of a pipe I could make out a brightly colored shawl embroidered with flowers, a stiff coiffe with a wing standing out, a round sunburned cheek, the gleam of silver jewelry.

At dusk, before supper and the dancing, these young, dark-haired Bigouden women would walk about in two's and three's, in a lazy, aimless way, as though they intended only to decorate the white sand and the violet-colored rocks with their flowered fichus and their stiff coiffes. In the hollow of a ditch, at the turning of a path fortified with prickly juniper bushes, they would suddenly appear, silent and hopeful, with the submissive, bantering air of young neutered animals. One moonlit night, when the calm sea was fringed with silver and the Kervilaouen lighthouse shone high up through a blue and intangible hoarfrost, one of the bolder ones dared to hail us in a respectful tone of voice:

"Don't you need anyone?"

"What for?"

"To go to bed with . . ."

We looked at her laughingly, amused by her shy audacity, her applelike face, her spinning-top blouse well pulled down beneath a little shawl as blue as the night. She was young, wearing a clean linen coiffe, and seemed freshly waxed and polished, while the slightest movement of her skirt swept toward us a revolting smell of stale fish. . . .

A strange dénouement crowned this cheerful holiday, and I'm overcome with helpless laughter when I remember our departure before the scandalized gaze of the people of Palais. I had given up not only shoes and stockings but feminine skirts, and Renaud could say what a nice cabin-boy his wife made, in her big blue collar, jersey trousers and woolen beret, a cabin-boy who quickly learned how to manage sails and proudly shortened the jib sail. One afternoon, in the hollow of a red and purple rock covered with a rough warm carpet of velvet lichen, Renaud rashly treated his ship's boy as a much-loved mistress, and two bathers who were passing unnoticed looked away—afterwards. The distance and the clothes, only slightly disarranged, had led those contemplative souls astray and my impatient husband became, for Palais society, who blushed in shame, the "revolting Parisian who seduces little ship's boys for forty sous or three francs!"

O slandered Renaud! How I relished your mixed expression before the critical gaze of Palais society, your triple expression of childish anger, amusement, and feminine modesty! But I, the ship's boy you had violated, I couldn't remove my trousers and blue jacket to let my splendid nudity restore your ruined reputation!

A piercing cry, the squeak of a mouse that someone stepped on, followed by strange rippling laughter, cut through my reverie. What was happening to Marcel —or Annie? I rushed to the darkroom, where that cry and laughter had come from, that hysterical laughter which stopped and started again. . . .

"Don't be shy, children. Tell me what you've been playing at."

Marcel came out of the darkroom, his eyes full of tears, and leaned against the corridor wall, with his hand on his heart.

"Oh, how silly!" he sobbed. "It'll give me hysterics, you know!"

"Why?"

"It's Annie . . . it was she who . . . oh, I know she didn't do it on purpose . . ."

"Annie? . . . what did she do?"

The accused came out of the darkroom in her turn, looking pale, her eyelashes fluttering, and began to talk like a sleepwalker:

"Honestly . . . I didn't do anything! He's got it wrong! I'm not capable of . . . anyhow, Claudine, don't believe it!"

Marcel threw back his head and sobbed with laughter, while I began to doubt Annie's honesty.

"Did she bully you, Marcel? Poor little boy, then! He looks like a crumpled rose. Come with your stepmother!"

I took him to my bedroom, putting my arm round his sloping shoulders. He was still shaking with nervous schoolboy laughter; he was so pathetic, so precious, and so silly that I didn't know whether I wanted to spank him or hug him even more fiercely.

I could feel behind me that Annie was trying to escape and vanish into the darkness of the corridor.

"Annie! What are you up to? Come and appear before me, and quickly!"

I was enjoying myself in a benevolent way, with just a hint of base curiosity in my pleasure. Annie stood there, her mouth half-open and trembling, looking like a version of the "broken vase" picture painted for mulattoes; she might have seemed the victim if Marcel, his blue eyes shining with nervous tears, had not claimed the most straightforward compassion. I sat in an easy chair, placed my hands on the arms and tried the case:

"Children, I'm listening. Marcel, tell me! What did Annie do?"

He entered into the spirit of the game and waggled his entire body, like Polaire. "She fondled me," he cried.

"*I* did?"

"Hush, Annie. . . . She fondled you! What do you mean by that?"

"Goodness, I mean what everyone means! Fondled, that's all!"

"Er—did she take your hand? Or put her arm round your waist?"

"Oh—"

"Silence, Annie, for goodness' sake! Your ear, your knee, your . . ."

"More or less everything," admitted Marcel, acting as though he'd lost the game.

"No, not everything!" cried Annie so impetuously that we both began to laugh helplessly.

Oh, how I love it! How good it feels to be young again over a bit of schoolchildren's silliness, to feel your ribs expanding, your cheeks go taut with laughter and your cheekbones shoot up to your eyes! I felt as I used to feel during evening school, that hour of extra study when a look exchanged with big Anaïs or a word spoken out of turn by Marie Belhomme sent a wave of irrepressible laughter through all the girls, the idiotic contagious delight of children who are shut up indoors. My childhood, how close to me you are this evening, and how far away!

And while Marcel and I laughed, Annie wept. She wept slowly as she stood there; she seemed so sad that I was upset, and my laughter slowed down into gurgles and stopped. I rushed over to her and took her by the shoulder.

"Darling, my silly little girl! Are you out of your mind? We're silly, I know, but you don't have to cry like that!"

She freed herself with a twist of her shoulders, a movement of her eyebrows and lips, a pale fleeting look which expressed so much! I was anxious and full of compassion; I understood completely what that look was saying: "No, I'm not crying out of spite, nor out of shame; I'm crying out of longing and disappointment. I'm crying for what I'm deprived of, for what escapes my hands and my mouth, for what I shall have to seek far away, or else very near. . . . I'll have to go myself, even though I'm tired, sedentary and lazy, even though I'm shy and passive, because I'm the slave of my greedy, obstinate body. I'll have to rush out in search of brief happiness that doesn't come to find me. . . . So I'll go, without gaiety and

178

without confidence, side by side with my desire that doesn't even possess a face, who has only a delightfully curved back, legs covered with tickly golden down, arms ready to embrace and quick to let go, a heart warm with impatience and ingratitude . . . I'll go! For I'm struggling in vain, and I've no longer any confidence in myself. Yes, alongside my desire, all the way along a burning path, I shall walk, proudly giving myself, submitting to my unworthy and dear companion—I foresee he will be unworthy, and I smile in advance at my blind choice which gropes its way with fingers outstretched. I shall go happily right to the turning where my treacherous guide will dissolve like the many-colored rainbow light which dances over the dew in the sunshine, and I'll find myself once more well-behaved, out of breath, fulfilled, deserted, alone with my little-girl naïveté that's been washed away by sin, sighing: 'I shan't do it again,' and I shall still turn toward the fading image of my impurity . . ."

I read all this in Annie's eyes, in the desolate water of her look. . . . And how I was tempted—was generous or licentious?—to throw Marcel into her arms, that delightful doll who looked like a man, just as one might secretly give some sort of shameful plaything to a prisoner. . . .

"Marcel . . ."

"Yes, dear friend?"

"Don't act the society woman: this is serious."

"I'm not acting the society woman, Claudine. Aren't you my dear friend?"

"I'm your stepmother, sir, even your old pal, an old pal you're very good at touching when it's necessary, and even when it's not!"

"You're hard . . ."

"No, my child. I don't reproach you over the louis that I've let myself be done out of now and then; I didn't mind at all. And the proof is that I might be able to offer you a splendid chance of getting hold of five louis—or ten, or fifteen, I can't say . . ."

"Oh ho, have you invented a beauty lotion? Or does some old man want to have me?"

"What a notion, dear boy! You're not an under-age pickup for elderly diplomats! No . . . Marcel, listen!"

"I'm listening."

"Haven't you ever, in the biblical sense of the word, *known* a woman?"

He gave me a frozen stare.

"Here are the smelling salts. I'll start again: Haven't you ever—"

"Never! I swear it!"

"That will do. Your blue eyes and your rose-pink voice proclaim your innocence. Now tell me this: If someone put into your bed a pretty woman who was in love with you, what would you do?"

"Nothing . . . and I shall go away. I don't want to hear obscenities!"

"And what if you were paid for it?"

"If I were—are you serious?"

"Very."

"Oh bother! Is some fat lady after me?"

"Not fat; she's slim. And she's nice!"

"Nice . . . I'm suspicious . . ."

He was suspicious, in fact, for I had got him cornered between two doors, in the round space, as deep as an alcove, which separates the dining room from the drawing room. He was suspicious, for I was insistent, with a sort of bogus lightheartedness which didn't take in that sly little creature; a conventional lightheartedness which seemed to emphasize our rapid replies by adding stage directions:

MARCEL (guardedly) . . .

CLAUDINE (irresponsibly) . . .

"Nice, nice. Can a woman be nice? You remind me—and it hurts—of a story which I've never told you, I was so ashamed."

"Go on then!"

"Two years ago, at Biarritz, I'd unearthed a very young Englishman, delightful but married, the wretch! Married and free to have the kind of love he fancied, provided his wife could do the same. She was a little fair-haired ogress, completely round, with a bottom like an apple when she wore her blue woolen trousers. And didn't she get it into her head, if I can use that expression, to have me! They got me drunk on whiskey, the devils, and then I was left alone with the little ogress who was determined to have everything! Oh, Claudine! That moment! I'm frightened when I think of it. Every nice thing that can be said or done to a good-looking boy, she lavished it all on me, and it was a terrible failure! From time to time hope returned to me . . ."

"Is that called hope? 'Hope glimmers like a piece of straw in the cowshed . . .'"

"I thought of him—he was drinking champagne, a magnum—in an adjoining bedroom . . . and then, dash it, I had to start all over again! In the end she hit me in a rage and threw me out."

"And did you find the charming husband with the magnum again?"

"I found him, under the table. You see . . ."

"But it wouldn't be the same sort of thing, Marcel!"

I put my mouth to his ear, for I was slightly embarrassed by what I was undertaking. I whispered, I whispered for a long time. I was choking with words, although it was hard to get them out. Marcel was terrified, refused, and tried to bargain! I almost gave orders, but my severity was mitigated with a thump on the back, like a rough hug from a horse trader. He hadn't entirely consented when I left him; I didn't want to hear his last hesitations. I closed behind us the door to the confessional, where we had just devised something so innocent and so shady. . . .

May God be my judge—if he has time! I thought I was doing right. My cherished possession, my reason for living, was going to be restored to me, and I only wanted to see that my obsessed young friend didn't go off on her own, like a beggar, along the roads all blue with half-melted snow, stained with patches of flinty mud and flanked by withered berries; I wanted her to enjoy herself to the full here, shut in behind her drawn curtains, with a pretty, sufficiently animated mannequin. I wanted her to return to her shy gaiety, to smile again like an ill-treated child, to recover her idle, graceful insouciance. Poor girl! What a miserable fiasco, and how angry she could be with me!

Two days ago, when the wind in the evening was dark and warm, smelling of thaw and a false promise of spring, we sat down to a substantial peasant dinner of bacon, chicken cooked in wine, and a mahogany-colored pudding soaked in old rum . . . I resolutely drank a treacherous, sugary Frontignan, and continually filled up glasses for Annie, who had no suspicions, and for Marcel, who was in the know, shivering and silent; but he emptied glass after glass as though he were drinking hemlock, all at one go, throwing back his head, his eyes full of resentment and apprehension. . . .

What an odd evening, between that half-intoxicated girl and that boy with the deceptive under-age look! I felt as light and blind as a soap bubble, gently bumping into everything. A generous soul, in love with love, the soul of some disinterested go-between was supporting my own, to be sure! And, when I had "finished off" Annie with a glass of punch, when I had conducted this ill-assorted, graceful couple up to the first floor and finally pushed Marcel and his turquoise pajamas into Annie's bedroom, I went to bed cheerfully, buoyed up with a noble feverish excitement innocent of any impurity. Precisely! A faint cry, heartfelt and affectionate, alarmed me, and I returned to the door that had closed upon our two lovers, if I dare use the expression. . . .

Leaning against the door, and feeling more maternal than inquisitive, I listened . . . nothing . . .

Yes! A frightened, voluble murmur in which I distinguished two voices—then nothing more. . . . Yes. A very low moan, but so full of heartbreak and disappointment. A moan so significant that I was not surprised to find my solitary self muttering something which, through the person of Marcel, was gravely offensive to the third sex. And then, once more, silence. And then Marcel's voice, which sounded breathless, and its tone was one of polite excuse. . . . I was shivering with cold and nervous laughter. I could foresee ridiculous failure, a shady parody of sexual pleasure, yes, but not Marcel's shameful exit as he rushed out of the bedroom and walked savagely over my bare feet, uttering an angry, hostile "Damn!" which told me everything. He was pale, his nostrils pinched and his lips red; his blue eyes had turned black, he almost knocked over my lamp and pushed me down the stairs.

"Claudine! Oh, you were there, were you? Do you find that entertaining? Odd sort of taste!"

I was secretly humiliated and began to give him a dressing-down: "Now listen, my boy, I do as I please! And then I'm the starter, as you know very well!"

"Starter! Starter! Really now! Your friend can start on her own if she wants to! I'm getting out of the way!"

I shook his arm in a fury.

"You've got a cheek, haven't you! What happened?"

"Nothing! Leave me alone! I'm going to bed."

He pulled himself free with a resentful schoolboy gesture and slipped along the corridor like an eel.

In her room, which I entered softly after knocking, my poor little Annie was crying into her crumpled pillow through the long strands of her black hair which she had not plaited. At first she turned away, but her angry silence, with clenched teeth and closed eyes, soon melted in my friendly arms. She was burning hot; she smelled of the sandalwood which had been thrown on the fire, and she sobbed wordlessly, exclaiming "Oh, oh" in a crushed voice, with sighs which made her whole body heave. She couldn't talk, and all I could see of her as she lay against my shoulder were her black swallowlike head with its streaming hair and two pathetic hands which masked her face. . . .

The soothing warmth of my arms brought her sad, brief story to the surface; it flowed drop by drop, along with her tears.

It consisted only of sighs, words interrupted and begun again, complaints which she didn't explain; but to me they were quite clear.

"Oh, he's so horrible, he's so horrible! It's your fault! Oh, it'll kill me! Oh, I'm so miserable! I want to go away, I never want to see him again . . . I was so happy! He looked so nice in blue! I felt right away that it wouldn't work, you know! So I closed my eyes, and I caressed him, so as not to lose him. But, you know, I'm so clumsy, it only made things worse. Oh, he's so horrible! He called me 'madame' . . . he said he was sorry, as though he'd stepped on my toe . . . just when I was dying of shame at having tried and failed. Honestly, Claudine, an insult would have been better. I want to go away: I'm too miserable! It's your fault, Claudine, it's all your fault . . ."

I knew that only too well, unfortunately! How could I console her? How could I make enough excuses for myself? This childish, disgusting plot, this bargaining with Marcel, I'd have liked to erase them. from my memory, take Annie in my arms and tell her "It was only a bad dream . . ."

I was filled with loving remorse; I nearly hugged Annie's pathetic little heaving body more closely, nearly tightened my straightforward embrace . . . caresses and kisses—wherever they came from—were the only way of curing and calming the sorrow of this ingenuous prostitute. My goodness, I admit, and may Renaud forgive me, the sacrifice would not have been too much for me. But with a little effort I remembered our years of chaste friendship, this gray winter which had brought us together under one peaceable roof—and also the Margravine's garden where Annie, who was in distress, offered herself to me so confidently. What good would it have done? For the sake of a few days, a few hectic nights scented with her warm smell of sandalwood and white carnations, I might have risked leaving the poor child sadder still. I didn't tighten my embrace, I only kissed her hair and her cheeks salty with tears; I opened the window to the warm dark wind, already laden with the joy of spring . . . I resorted to orange-blossom water and a hot-water bottle for her slim, cold feet—and I went away, displeased with myself, planning immediate exile for Marcel. . . .

At luncheon Marcel and I found ourselves alone, seated opposite each other, hostile and embarrassed. Annie had remained in her room. In fact my charming stepson seemed less uncomfortable than I was, but I concealed my embarrassment beneath an extremely bad grace. He talked, with feigned, timid politeness. He was rather pale, wearing a gray suit with a tie of the same blue as the pajamas he had worn the previous night. . . .

"It's a lovely day today, isn't it, Claudine? It's really springlike!"

"Yes. Good weather for traveling. You'll take advantage of it, won't you?"

"Me? but . . ."

"Yes, yes, you will. It's an exceptional opportunity, and you know that the four o'clock train goes straight through?"

He looked at me, undecided: "But—the four o'clock train is an express which takes only first-class passengers, and my means hardly allow me . . ."

"I'll see to that . . ."

In spite of my grumpy tone of voice he lowered his eyelids and ventured to smile like some bitchy little girl:

"Oh, how kind you are . . . and in fact you owe it to me: I really suffered last night!"

I wanted to spank him and was thinking that if I promised him fifty francs more he'd get a thrashing, when the door opened and Annie appeared. She must have made an effort, and the strain she had imposed on her will-power lit up her pale sleepwalker's eyes.

I threw down my napkin and ran over to her:

"You shouldn't have come down, Annie! Why did you?"

"I don't know—I felt hungry. I get bored all on my own . . ."

And in her anguish she smiled a society type of smile which was completely out of place.

"Sit down. Marcel was just telling me he's leaving."

"Oh?"

Her pale eyes rolled to one side, showing the whites, which were periwinkle blue. We had to hurry!

"Yes, he's leaving at four. You're sorry, I see?"

"Yes," she replied faintly. "He could have stayed until his father arrived."

"Obviously," agreed Marcel politely.

Why should he interfere? I was angry, for I was in the wrong:

"If you think your father will be pleased! You can easily see that Annie's not well, she needs rest, she must be on her own . . ."

In reply to this unfortunate phrase I received a look of such pointed irony that I lost my sang-froid:

"And in any case, damn it all, I've had enough! Yes, I'm in the wrong, yes, I've interfered in something that doesn't concern me, and I'm asking my dear Annie with all my heart to forgive me; it was worse than a blunder, it was a bad deed. But you, you poisonous creature, I don't owe you anything—only your ticket to Paris, and get out, because—"

"Oh my goodness, I can't bear scenes! I'm off!"

Deliberately, with that twist of the hips which is his personal specialty, my stepson rose, in spite of a timid and spontaneous gesture from Annie as though to follow him or stop him. The door banged after him and the old staircase creaked under his light step. . . .

We were alone. I felt guilty and unkind, and my skin felt tight, as though I were running a fever. I was thirsty. I didn't dare look at Annie, but I could see the lace on her negligee quivering from the beating of her heart. A faint sigh forced me to look up at her face, which was brown and long like a ripe almond, and unhappiness did not disturb its unchanging outline.

"So there," she murmured, sighing again.

And I repeated her words:

"So there . . ."

She enveloped me with a long blank look and moaned softly: "What's left for me now?"

I felt hurt for no reason and replied harshly: "The four o'clock train, if you want. Or else the gardener's son. Marcel thought highly of him."

She blushed slowly; successive waves of pink suffused her brown cheeks and her delicate little ears.

"I had thought of it," she admitted naïvely, without resentment. "But I think a change of air abroad would be more suitable."

Thank goodness, she was herself again! I wanted to cry and laugh and clasp her in my arms, for the intense pleasure of finding her intact and like herself again, not even grazed by real sorrow, as immodest as Péronnelle in heat, and yet attached to superficial conventions, ready to unfasten her dress for a stranger but shyly calling out to me "Don't come in!" when she was merely washing her face in her bedroom. . . .

Thank goodness, I need hardly reproach myself for anything! I'm happy again, I can selfishly prepare in my heart for Renaud's return, tremble with happiness and regret as I see the sticky lilac buds adventurously shooting up, and say to myself: "Spring's already on the way! How many days have gone by without him!" I can listen to my blood tingling in my fingertips and around the warm rims to my ears; I can feel a thrill, I can remember, hope and believe, in my forgetful yet faithful memory, that yesterday is tomorrow, that

I'm seventeen and he's thirty-nine, and this is the first time in my life I've waited for him. . . .

So let Annie go quietly—to be loved somewhere else! She runs, she rushes, while I wait. We're both vagabonds, and if our slightest thoughts separate us, then what strange friendship, made up of pity, despotism, weakness and irony still brings us together? She doesn't envy me, and I pity her only at certain moments of crisis. She recounts her thoughts just as a stream overflows; I remain silent through pride and modesty. She yields her body ardently, her skin that is soft and warm as the oiled marble where delicate dough is kneaded—and the down all over my body stands on end when I merely think of an unknown man's embrace, and it is she, so weak and gentle, who shocks and astonishes me. . . .

What then keeps me close to her? What then makes me tolerate, even sometimes want her silent presence, her defeated attitude, her useless little hands? Why then do I call her, to myself, "my poor Annie"?

It's because she wanders about, searching, needing what I, once and for all, have found.

"What's left for me now?"

Annie's feeble cry, her resigned, plaintive, unde-manding sigh, how it rises bitterly to my lips! But I'm not resigned, and I rebel, and I draw myself up again, ready to invoke goodness knows what imagi-nary rights. Imaginary! I look around me, astonished that the whole background to my happiness does not collapse, like a moving fantasy, beneath my gaze.

Yes, Renaud has returned! He's there, in the next room, so close that I can hear his breathing, the slight rustle of the book he's glancing through. He's there, and he's no longer himself—or else I'm no longer Claudine. . . .

"He'll come back," I used to say to myself, "and that day the dusk will be as light as a moonlit night: The mere outline of his shadow framed in the railway carriage door will allow me to recognize my entire beloved past, all my present love . . ."

Heavens! What nightmare did I begin to live through a week ago? Why didn't I recognize his voice, or his look, or the warmth of his embrace? I entrusted to those men who took him away to the snow an invalid who was exhausted but so alive, a nervous overworked man who was still capable of reacting; what right had they to send me back an old man?

An old man, an old man! . . . is it possible? My friend, my lover, my companion during those hours when we heard no other sound save our own breathing, crushed one against each other—I ask you, is it possible? And if it really is, if you are no more than a loving shadow by my side, a pale and stooping image of my love, what aberration forbade me to see in advance what is happening now? I'm twenty-eight, you're fifty, and your young middle age was so brilliant, so impatient and so proud that I hoped more than once, oh my love; I wished to see you calmer at fifty. Fatal wish, heard by some ironic god! All at once there you are, magically, irreparably in accordance with my rash hope: an old man! The dark pools of your eyes are dulled, withered is the mouth where mine found its caress, and those fine strong arms are now limp as they embrace me! Oh, who is punishing me, and why? Here I am in tears; my hands are empty, just like Annie who was crying, just here, for the most tangible, the basest form of love. Here I am, with all my strength which has never been used to the full; here I am, young, punished and deprived of what I secretly love with ardent fervor, and I'm naïvely wringing my hands at my disaster, before the mutilated image of my happiness. The man I used to call "my father" as part of a filial love-game, now, for the rest of our lives, has become my grandfather.

He loves me and suffers in silent humiliation, for I don't want what he offers me, and I accept neither his gentle skilled hands nor his mouth to which I owed so many delights. My nerves and my sense of shame refuse to imagine him in this role of a complaisant and insensitive instrument . . .

He's there, in the room next door, anxious about my presence and my silence. He wants to call me and dares not. The moment he returned I could read on his pale lips his wish to ask a question, to have an explanation. But I'm evasive. I consent to suffer— but not to listen to him. We tell heroic lies with cheerful smiles, as though we were strangers. I'm going to start humming now, for I can hear him think, and I can feel that if I don't speak, if I don't sing, if I don't move my chair, he'll call me. I prefer to suffer in a guilty way; I'm as impatient with my grief as with a burn that hurts unbearably when I'm alone; but I lie to him, with all the serenity of my face and eyes, with all the inoffensive caress of my mouth, for I don't want him to talk, to lower himself to make excuses which will leave me more humiliated than him; I don't want him to offer me some kind of abdication that I would never, never accept. I'm refusing my liberty! I look at it with an affectionate disdain, like a plaything from my childhood days; and besides, perhaps I wouldn't know what to do with it now. . . .

And then, even when my grief is most intense, during the hours of the night when I delicately carve out for myself the place that hurts me most, with that idiotic kind of pride which could have led me in the past to bite my own tongue as I smiled—at the height of those exhausting gymnastics through which I train my will-power—is there not an obstinate, almost unconscious hope, like the hope of a plant shaken by the storm, obscurely waiting for the end of the squall? Is there not already a confident voice whispering: "It will come right. I don't know how, but it will come right. There's no irreparable sorrow, save death. The mere habit of living uncomfortably, of suffering every day, this passive routine is already a remedy, a rhythm which modifies and sweetens the hours that pass. . . .

"People don't die of anything," declared Marthe in a penetrating voice, "and certainly not of grief! Nobody dies of grief! Look at Claudine, now—when Renaud died, everyone said to one another: 'It'll kill her, you can be sure!' And, thank goodness, it didn't! She's got too much common sense, really, she enjoys life too much."

I smiled out of politeness, looking toward the garden, turning away from the smoke that Marthe was exhaling, her cheeks full of it. She had aged too, but her striking makeup concealed the fact. Even when motoring she didn't abandon the bright colors which emphasized the red-gold of her hair and the whiteness of her skin. A long, long green veil encircled her narrow toque, and she'd thrown into an armchair the purple tussah topcoat which protected her saffron-colored dress. I thought she looked smaller, rounder, more tense; her bosom was thrust forward and her croup obvious. And her entire mobile face rebelled, with the aggression of the fashionable incendiarist that she was, against the necessity for growing old, getting fat, and coming to an end.

This morning a red-and-yellow sixty horsepower car deposited at the bottom of my unsteady black stone steps Maugis, white with dust and red with heat, Léon Payet as the chauffeur, wearing goggles, and his wife. Annie followed, pleased to see me again but embarrassed because she dared not say so. They came noisily into my silent house, and I could only let them come in, sit down and have luncheon, for solitude has made me shy and slow to express myself.

Maugis puffed and sweated, drinking big glasses of water and small glasses of fine champagne. The heat overpowered him, and he could hardly do any more than clasp my hands within his own, which were clammy, saying: "Well then, my old pal!"—words in which I could read his affectionate drunken memories. Marthe fanned herself, and her husband, who was bearded, well turned out, ridiculous and unhappy, digested his meal. My little Annie, sitting in

Marthe's shadow, disturbed me; she was far off, so like the Annie of old times, so submissive to Marthe's dry words that I didn't know what to think.

I'm patient; I tolerate these people. They'll leave this evening, when the sun goes down. Their tormented images will have passed briefly over my peaceful dream. I await their departure with the resignation of a guest, and from time to time I look down at my brown peasant hands, folded in my lap. I smile, I talk a little. I look toward the garden, through the gleaming doorway where the flies create a delicate network of silvery wings. My familiar pets have fled in discreet self-defense, but I can hear Toby lurking about on the gravel path, the voice of Prrou, my ginger cat, calling me, for she's bored, and the friendly call of Ziasse, my magpie. . . .

Despite the drawn venetian blinds, I can see my reflection in the dark water of the mirror facing me; it has no place among those of Marthe, Maugis, and the two others—my dark reflection, dressed in white, my unadorned and tangled hair that the sun bleaches like that of a shepherdess. . . . I'm waiting for them to leave.

I wait patiently. I'm used to it now. I know that no day is interminable, that even nights when you toss feverishly, rebelling against grief, the clammy sheets, the ticking of the clock; even these nights come to an end. They'll go soon, these people who've disturbed me, making luminous rings on the water of my pool. They talk a lot, especially Marthe. They tell me about Paris and watering places; they stop short, impatient at my silence: "Did you know, now?"—hurl names at me to make me remember, like a rope thrown to a drowning man who's floundering. I say: "Oh, yes . . ." in a conciliatory way, and then I leave them once again.

The bar of sunlight moves across the floor slowly, slowly but surely. In the same way it settles and moves down there, against the espalier wall, over the pink cheek of my finest peach. Let's listen to what these people are saying, sitting there in front of big misted glasses full of trembling raspberry syrup diluted with cool water. They're not talking discreetly. They're talking about me as though I were someone who was asleep beside them. . . .

"She looks wonderfully well, Maugis, don't you agree?"

"Yes and no. She's seasoned like a good hunting saddle. Gone over with walnut stain, as you might say. It suits her."

"I don't find any change in her," said Marthe, going one better.

"*I* do," murmured Annie.

"Her eyes are more expressive," stated Léon Payet, although nobody had asked his opinion.

"She's perhaps a little less lively," remarked Marthe. "But on the whole, see, country life doesn't cause as much harm as you think. I must try one of these sunshine treatments that there's so much talk about. Shall we see you in Paris this winter, Claudine? You know I've got a lovely bedroom for you."

"Oh, thank you, Marthe . . . no, I don't think so."

She gave me a look like a whiplash, rapid and friendly.

"Come, my dear! you have to accept the inevitable! One must pick up, you know! It will be eighteen months this winter since we lost our poor friend. One must make an effort, for goodness' sake! Isn't that true, Maugis? You're all looking at me! Surely I'm right?"

"Yes, certainly," agreed Annie timidly.

But Maugis shrugged his plump shoulders.

" 'Make an effort, make an effort!' Leave her alone! I don't know how you can think of any effort that isn't directed toward an absinthe, with this weather!"

I smiled in order to do something. These people were deciding on my fate, discussing what I did as though I were a black slave up for sale. Then I rose.

"Come with me, Annie, you can help me pick some roses for you and Marthe."

And I led her away, taking her by the arm, while Marthe accompanied us with an aggressive remark:

"That's it, children: Off you go and tell your little secrets!"

A mantle of warmth fell about our shoulders, and I fled, pulling down the blinds behind me, as far as the lake of cool shade which lay spread out beneath the old walnut tree. Annie was behind me, her hands idle. Her brown skin showed through her lawn blouse, its texture close and shiny, like a silken lining. She was silent and surveyed with a kind of literary melancholy my ruined and luxuriant domain, the garden which was no longer a garden, the wall which the powerful roots from the walnut tree had first damaged and then pulled down, until it showed the russet, almost burnt color at the back of the stones. The rose tree with the flesh-pink roses was dead, too. It had died from flowering too much. A nimble honeysuckle had greedily stifled my delicate clematis which rained down in mauve stars, so big and soft. The ivy had replaced the wistaria; it was twisting the gutter and padding the roof which it was scaling, and, since it could find no further room to climb, stretched out a strong twisted arm toward the sky, spiked with green seeds and a hum of bees. . . .

"There aren't any flowers," murmured Annie.

I looked at her gently and took her hand.

"Yes, there are, Annie. In the low garden."

Down the unkempt walks, beneath the Virginia creeper which avidly held out its curling tendrils toward us, I led her to the low garden, a warm terrace-type priest's garden, as you might say, where I tended my common flowers: phlox made violet by the sunshine, aconites of a watery blue, marigolds as round and golden as mandarins, fine French marigolds, brown and yellow like velvety hornets ruched with a goffering iron, each tightly held within its bursting calyx. Along the espalier wall a curtain of rose bushes protects the feet of the peach and apricot trees, and as I go past my eyes lovingly feel the apricots which are already ripe, while the sun enhances their smooth flesh with black beauty spots.

"Don't prick yourself, Annie; I've got some pruning shears. No, those are too far out. You'll have the tea roses, they're the best ones. Do you like them?"

Annie's blue eyes became moist. It was her way of blushing.

"Oh yes, Claudine. How kind you are!"

"I'm not kind, my child. I think these roses suit you very well, that's all."

She took from my hands the roses I held out to her, their stems uppermost, so that the heavy flower heads wouldn't lose their petals. She pricked her finger, became embarrassed and tried to say something. I smiled at her attempts, but I no longer helped her as I used to do.

"How kind you are, Claudine!" she repeated. "I didn't expect to find you like this."

"Why?"

"I was a terrible coward about seeing you again; I was afraid of seeing your grief and surprising you in tears. The mere idea of it made me think of running away, just anywhere. . . . Marthe made me feel ashamed . . ."

"Marthe is always tactful . . ."

She brightened and dared to look me in the face.

"Oh, you're talking just as you used to talk. I'm glad! I'm so surprised, Claudine, not to find you more—"

"More sad?"

She signified yes, and I attempted to indicate my apologies, like someone who understands his mistake but can do nothing about it. Annie was thinking, as she removed the hard, curved thorns, shaped like tiger's claws, from one rose stem. She assumed an air of reserved compunction and finally asked:

"Where is Renaud's grave, Claudine?"

With my shoulder I indicated an invisible spot toward the west.

"Over there, in the cemetery."

And I sensed that I had shocked her. Renaud's grave—that miniature enclosure surrounded with a painted iron grill, its white flat stone stained by rainstorms . . . I look after it in a constrained, cold way. Nothing about it makes me sad, nothing keeps me there. Nothing remains beneath that tomb of the one I love, the one of whom I still say, within my heart: "He *says* this . . . he *prefers* that . . ." A tomb is only an empty box. The one I love exists entirely in my memory, in a handkerchief that's still scented when I unfold it, in an intonation that I suddenly remember and listen to for a whole long moment, my head bent. He exists in a short loving note, where the handwriting will grow faint, in a worn old book caressed by his eyes, and his figure will always be seated, for me—but only for me—on that bench from where he would pensively watch the Montagne aux Cailles grow blue in the twilight. . . . What need was there to speak?

"Take this red rose, Annie. Marthe can pin it on her green veil, or her yellow dress."

She took it without a word. A crazy bee flew by, passing so close to her mouth that she drew back and wiped her lips with the back of her hand.

"Don't be frightened. It's a bee on its way home. Their nest's inside the wall that's fallen down. . . ."

I indicated it with my shoulder, as I had done earlier for the cemetery, and Annie's look was critical again. I didn't lose my temper; I felt old and kind-hearted, in front of a child who couldn't understand. . . .

Something reddish-brown rushed out from the dwarf rosebushes, the ones that were weighed down with yellow unscented roses. It leapt into the sunshine, shot away and disappeared. It was a silly game being played by Prrou, my ginger cat, my mild, crazy creature . . . I laughed out loud at Annie's fright.

"Do you know who that is, Annie? It's Prrou. And Prrou's the daughter of Péronnelle!"

"Péronnelle? Oh, have you still got her?"

Her eyes became moist once more; she was thinking of the year when she went off again, leaving me Toby and the gray cat. . . .

"I still have her. She's getting rather old and sleeps a lot. Among other misdeeds she produced this fox-colored daughter whom I call Prrou. Can you see her?"

Between two branches of weeping acacia a ferocious face was watching us, sandy and leonine, with green-amber eyes. We could see the broad nose, the prominent chin and the cheeks as muscular as those of a wild beast.

"She looks very fierce."

"She *is* rather fierce. She kills hens, attacks tom-cats, eats birds, and scratches the cook. I can hardly ever get hold of her myself, but she always follows me at a distance, even into the woods. She avoids everything and is frightened of nothing. She's rather like Marthe, don't you think?"

"You're right," agreed Annie, amused.

"I was rather surprised, Annie, you know, to see the two of you together again."

Annie became upset, pricked herself on the roses she was carrying, and sucked a drop of blood from her finger.

"Yes, I know it might seem odd to you . . . Marthe was so insistent, she was so kind about wanting to have me with her and bring me on this motoring expedition . . ."

"Does the car belong to her?"

"Yes—that is—it's partly mine too . . . I paid for half of it."

"Oh, I see . . ."

"And then—how silly one can be!—old habits are incredibly strong. In front of Marthe I find myself such a little girl again, so much 'whatever-you-say.' She's so much stronger than I am . . ."

I seized her hand. "But my poor child, are you attached again?"

The same attractive, mysterious smile that she used to have passed over her face.

"Oh, attached . . . attachments get broken off, as you well know . . ."

"That's all to the good, Annie!"

"It's nice of you to go on looking after me a bit," she murmured submissively. "I was feeling shy at finding you so different from what I'd imagined . . ."

"But why, my child? Admit it, did you want to find me with prematurely white hair, and all muffled up in crepe?"

"Oh, don't talk like that," she cried. "Yes, I wanted to find you changed, destroyed, like a shadow of your former self . . ."

Her arms opened, all the roses fell down and surrounded her with a sentimental and graceful disorder.

"I thought you would be stricken and ill, dragging out your life and hating it, detesting everything that breathed and flourished, in fact! And here you are, young and lively, among animals and bees . . . what's the use of love, that great love you were so proud of, Claudine? When such a love is over, can you go on living? Or else it wasn't love!"

Her outburst was sincere. She had loved me, and she was indignant that I should decline in her eyes; that I could, after Renaud, forget, flower again. Should I, for her, emerge from my silence which doesn't condescend to explain itself? No. I couldn't tolerate that any bitter water should rise from the sleeping depths of my calm sorrow and reach my eyes, or make my lips tremble. I bent down, picked up the scattered roses and crammed them into my friend's hands.

"Yes, my child, it was love! You can be certain it was, and leave with that certainty. It was the finest love, the love that lives its own life and continues after life. Console yourself, my child, I haven't lost my love! Believe what I say, or else that my reason is failing slightly, it doesn't matter . . ."

She shook her head to hide the tears she couldn't wipe away, for her arms were full of flowers. Upright and flower-laden, she wept; she was like a plant in the rain. It was I who consoled her, I who put my arms around her. And I don't know whether my sad smile was for her, or for me. . . .

A little black bull terrier, no longer very young, and slightly plump, rushed like a bull toward us and raised his muzzle. He looked like a little Japanese monster and was anxious because our faces, with their tears and kisses, were so close together. . . .

"Toby, Toby—it's Toby!"

"Well yes, Annie, it's Toby. Why shouldn't it be Toby?"

"I don't know . . . I didn't think that all these pets would live so long, Claudine . . ."

"So long . . . it's only two and a half years since you gave them to me! And only eighteen months since Renaud died."

"That's true . . ."

She shuddered and cast a frightened look toward the big black house which could be seen above us, over the rank vegetation in the upper garden.

"Did he—did he die here?" she murmured in a terrified voice.

"Naturally . . . in our bedroom. You can see the window, the one that's wide open . . ."

"And do you still sleep in that room, Claudine?"

"Oh yes!"

I uttered my reply so fervently that she looked at me, her mouth half-open.

"I'd be frightened . . . oh yes, I'd be frightened! He wasn't confined to bed very long, was he?"

"Mercifully no, darling. A week or ten days, I think . . . I didn't count them."

"Oh, it makes no difference, I would always see him lying there . . . don't *you* see him, then?" She went pale, looking gray, like a mulatto. She nursed her nervous fear in a childish way, and cultivated her little shudders.

Absentmindedly I stroked her brown shoulder, which could be seen through the transparent lawn of her blouse.

"No, darling, I don't."

I slowly prolonged my thoughts, which I didn't express. Annie would be offended, once again, at knowing that this unexpected image of Renaud lying in bed, overcome and half-petrified by the sudden attack of paralysis fades so quickly within me . . . I reject that vision, I eliminate it as one does a photograph that has gone wrong. Sometimes I see again, in an obsessive way, his tall body lying covered by the white sheet . . . but I quickly turn that page, I leaf through the rich album of our life; I admire luminous views from which no detail, no color is missing—not a fold from the clothes he was wearing at the time, not a single blue gleam from

his deep gaze—a handsome portrait that I caress on
purpose, framed by the gold of a magnificent hour.

"Yoo-hoo!"

The strident voice of some Valkyrie riding over
the clouds tore us away from our various dreams.
Marthe, elegant, green and yellow, was coming toward us, with Maugis in her wake, dragging his leg,
for he was already suffering from ataxia. From a distance she still looked like a Helleu. From near at
hand, the collaboration of some inferior Fournery became more obvious. She was waving one of her long-
gloved hands in the air and shouted as she walked.

"Well then, you two over there; are those secrets
finished now? Children, there's nothing to be done
about it, we must think about moving off. Léon's
under the car; he's mending some little thing; he
looks like a dog that's been run over."

Annie was watching her approach, a mingled expression on her little slave-girl face. She wanted to
stay with me, but she was afraid of my grief and
my solitude, which were both equally dear to me.
She was afraid of her sister-in-law and was yield-
ing in advance to the necessity of having an argu-
ment, fighting and making a decision. . . .

"I say, what beautiful roses! They're marvelous.
They won't fade between here and Auxerre, will
they, Claudine? We're going to stay the night at
Auxerre, you know. It's quite near, only fifty kilo-

meters away. There are two nasty hills, though! Maugis will have to walk up them, that'll make him lose weight."

He looked at her like an angry crab and was going to make some coarse reply when the kindhearted Annie, submissive as some would-be young girl, kindly placed a flower in the buttonhole of her alcoholic friend's white jacket; it was a jacqueminot rose, just opening, its dark velvety color tinged, at the curling edge of the petals, with silver—smooth enough to tempt our lips. Maugis bent down to look at the rose, creasing his double chin.

"Thank you, dear child. It's like you, scented and dark, a sister to you . . ."

Annie's gesture shocked me. This pseudo-filial kindheartedness, this shyness which made advances . . . O my little Annie of the past, I don't want to know why, in the deafening, dusty roar of this big red and yellow motorcar, you're following this couple who are united by chance and separated by hatred and disdain—and this big man who's been ruined by alcohol, a goodhearted man perhaps, but there's a kind of paternal vice about his feelings for you.

They were all hurrying now, active and talkative, rushing quickly around me as though I were a tree. The authoritative Marthe uttered brief commands from beneath the green veils which concealed her. She thought of the rugs, of her ever-present handbag, and asked the state of the headlight, while Léon

Payet, smoothly polite and gasoline-stained, executed her orders like a well-trained footman. This plump little woman inspired terror. She threw three coats and a rug over Annie's arm at random and came boldly toward me, holding up her skirt with two fingers through her coat, to offer me her veiled cheeks, her hooded, phantomlike little nose and her obstinate chin.

Maugis countered her talkative authority with a splendid power of inertia. His idle hands sank unto huge pockets, his cap came down over his eyebrows, a funnel-like collar reached up to his ears; he dug himself in, retired into his shell, asserting himself to be as useless and grumpy as a hedgehog.

I had a slight headache. From time to time I had the impression that I wasn't there, that I was asleep, that these people didn't exist . . . Annie too had shrouded herself in dust-colored muslin; Léon Payet glared at me through globular spectacles. . . . This nightmare oppressed me. What were these eyeless people doing near me, speaking to me with blind faces? Annie's blue eyes shone last, plaintive and ir-resolute. A harnessed thunderstorm roared at the foot of the mossy steps. I heard cries of "Good-bye, good-bye! . . . we'll see you soon!" "You never can tell . . . life is short. . . . Give way to temptation . . ." I felt leather paws take hold of my hands and shake them. Veils and goggles touched my cheeks and lips; my nervous anxiety increased. O Peer Gynt at the mercy of the Trolls! . . . Again I heard "Good-bye, good-bye, see you again . . ." and then shouts: "Annie, Annie, what has she forgotten now? . . ." Mechanically I went back to the drawing room which had been turned upside down by their presence, and all at once a slim form, mysterious beneath its dust-colored crepe, rushed up to me, arms embraced and enveloped me, a gentle, concealed voice murmured: "Good-bye, Claudine! Don't forget me. Help me, pick me up if ever I fall at your feet like a dead bird. Show me the pity you give to animals . . . pray to fate that when I've taken all the wrong directions I'll collapse on the road to your house . . ." Before I could return her embrace, my poor little lost creature had fled, and the red and yellow jaws of the motorcar engulfed the girl who had been my beloved vagabond. . . .

They've gone. Lacking the strength to restore calm and order to my house, I fall into a chair. How exhausting it has been, talking, listening, directing my eyes toward those active eyes, those agitated lips. Marthe's gestures are still going around noisily in my head. These dirty, empty glasses, these chairs out of place—you might think a band of revelers had passed this way; and Marthe's heady scent lingers here, commonplace and persistent . . .

Fan me, O my flowering lime tree, with the breath of your yellow crest, encircled with bees, fan me with your perfume in which orange blossom and vanilla are mingled. Stir up this air laden with tobacco and the smell of powdered women! Evening comes after a fine, hot, clear day, and weighs gently down over me. My blood becomes calmer and throbs less fiercely in my temples; they are cooler now.

Seated at the entrance to the garden, I relish my solitude with deep sighs, as though I'd been afraid of losing it . . .

They've gone, anxious little bull terrier who didn't recognize your former mistress; chattering, thieving Ziasse, limping along with your clipped wings ornamented with gay half-mourning; and you, ginger cat appearing on top of the wall like a lioness against the sky that's turning green—they've gone, we're alone. Alone, with the ghost who protects me, the ghost of the one I love. It was only a warning, my silent friends. Let's take up our life again, our full life which goes by with brief monotony. I begin to think again slowly. I think of Renaud, who used to lean his shoulder against this stone where I'm leaning now. If I turned around slightly, I could smile at him . . . but what would be the use? I can see him just as clearly without turning around . . . I stop thinking about him and remember the yellow peaches, threatened by the dormice. Which shall I spare, the pink and yellow peaches, or the velvety dormice, with their black and white tails, delightful and inoffensive? Oh, well, we'll see. . . . Come here, Toby, sit by my knees! Come and play this cruel game that I devised for the two of us last year, when

216

the one whom I called "your father" departed. I would say to you aloud: "Where's your father?" and your heartbroken affection—for you understand what cannot be remedied—burst out in shrill cries and big tears which streaked your fine toadlike eyes. . . . Answer me: Where's your father? You hesitate, your nose swells and you utter a gentle moan; you're not very convinced. Soon you won't know how to cry anymore . . . you'll forget. . . .

Shall I forget, I who saw him die? Shall I forget the moment when a terrifying stillness took him away from me, before he died? I can forget the resignation in his eyes, already relieved of living, sure of dying, and above all his hands, his feminine hands which paralyze, mercifully petrified in their familiar pose, the right one half-closed over an absent fountain pen, the left elegant and idle, the little finger separate from the others . . . Shall I lose the memory of that dark day when his imprisoned form, almost dead already, still struggled imperceptibly, with the impotent quivering of an entangled insect? With all my strength, my muscles tense, I involuntarily helped in his deliverance, I clenched my fists, I forgot myself so far as to say to the doctor: "Oh, I beg you, give him something to make him die more quickly!" The good man's astonished look hardly brought me back to my senses. . . .

Ah, here's my faithful bat! On finding me seated every evening on the steps, every evening she comes down a little lower and almost touches my hair. She swims, shrieks, rises again, snaps at the invisible, and touches my shoulder when I try to find her up in the air.

An arched back rubs against my legs, goes away, comes back, rubs against me again. There's a gentle purring from the ground, and it's the fat, striped Péronnelle coming to give me her evening greetings. In the twilight she seems transparent and tangible beneath her summer coat, like a gray shrimp in sea water. The reassuring night gathers around about me the circle of my animal friends, and all those I can't see in the dusk, but whose mysterious footsteps I can hear: the *tap-tap* of the hedgehog who trots adventurously from cabbage to rose, from rose to basket of peelings—a light sound on the gravel, the sound of something dragging a leg: it's the slow walk of the very old toad, the big, opulent toad who lives beneath the stones of the fallen wall. Toby's afraid of him, but Péronnelle is not beneath giving a timid scratch to his grainy back with the tip of one teasing paw. On the rose laurel a hawk moth is quivering, motionless, attached to the flower by his proboscis, as though it were very fine wire. He's transparent and quivers so violently that he seems to be his own shadow. Not long ago I wouldn't have resisted the temptation to take hold of him and enclose his electric flight within my hand, in order to see his phosphorescent eyes shining far from the lamp. I know better now; I cherish around about me the life of plants and unsuspecting creatures, and I want them to be free. . . .

A distant motorcar horn disturbs our silence, and Toby and Péronnelle prick up their ears. I reassure them: "They've gone . . ." Yes, they've really gone! "Oh, these great sorrows! You see what happens! Our Claudine's taking it easy; she looks very prosperous. The provinces have got something to offer, you know. They help . . ." And Annie is protesting, shocked at feeling the suspicion slowly enter her head—shocked and ready to understand, to forgive a weakness that would make me so like herself. The suspicion slowly enters her head as night falls; it pleases her, she remembers my coldness when speaking of Renaud's grave—she searches beneath the luxuriant and flowerless greenery of my garden for the adolescent figure of some young gardener. "Young bodies . . . heaven protect you, Claudine, from that temptation that's worse than the others! . . ." she used to say.

I'm afraid of no one, not even myself! Temptation? I know it. I live with it, it's becoming familiar and inoffensive. It's sunshine in which I soak myself, the mortal coldness of the evenings whose caress takes my shoulders by surprise, burning thirst which makes me run to the dark water where I see the quivering reflection of my lips joined to my real lips—energetic hunger which collapses with impatience. . . .

The other temptation, the flesh, whether the body is young or not? . . . Everything is possible; I'm waiting for it. It can't be terrible, desire without love. It is self-contained, it punishes and disperses itself. No, I'm not afraid of it; I'm no longer a child whom it can take by surprise, nor an old maid who's excited at its mere approach. I'll arm myself with all the unused energy which throbs so quietly in my veins. I'll arm myself with it against this common enemy. At each victory I'll call to witness the one who leans invisibly against the stone behind me, and whom I see without turning around; I'll say to him: "You see? How easy it is . . ."

Night comes down, closing quickly over this garden whose rich vegetation remains dark in the sunshine. The dampness of the earth rises to my nostrils: a smell of mushrooms, vanilla, and orange blossom . . . you might think that an invisible gardenia, feverish and white, is opening its petals in the darkness, it's the very aroma of this dew-drenched night . . . it's the breath, from beyond the gate and the moss-covered alley, of the woods where I was born, the woods which have taken me back. I belong to them again, now that their shade, their stifling silence, or their murmuring rain no longer disturb him who followed me as a stranger, soon tired, anxious beneath their vault of leaves; he who looked for the way out, the open air, the horizons swept with clouds and wind. . . . When I'm solitary I love the woods and they cherish me, because I'm solitary. Yet if the echo, on ground that's springy and carpeted with russet-brown pine needles, sometimes accompanies my step, I don't hasten it, and I take care not to turn my head . . . perhaps *he's* there, behind me, perhaps *he's* followed me, and his arms are outstretched to protect the track before me and disentangle the branches. . . .

My beloved sorrow is the dark and subtly colored hanging, the velvet beyond price that lines the interior of my heart. Harmless worries, unimpressive daily joys find their place there, in ephemeral fashion. Renaud's absence—Annie can criticize me for it and Marthe can laugh—doesn't prevent a little dog, for whom I am the only resource, from innocently asking for his food, his dish of water and his walk; nor a friendly cat from playing with the hem of my mourning dress, nor a world of plants from languishing and dying if I deprive them of my care. And what bitterness at first—but what calm relief later!—to discover, one day when spring still trembles with cold, uneasiness and hope—that nothing has changed: neither the smell of the earth, nor the quiver of the brook, nor the shape, like rosebuds, of the chestnut shoots. . . . To lean down in astonishment over the little filigree cups of the wild anemones, toward the carpet of endless violets—are they mauve, are they blue?—to let one's gaze caress the unforgotten outline of the mountains, to drink with a sigh of hesitation the piquant wine of a new sun . . . to live again! To live again with a touch of shame, then with more confidence, to find strength again, to find even the presence of the absent one in all that's intact, inevitable, unforeseen and serene in the march of the hours, the backdrop of the seasons. . . .

Two winters have already brought me shivering to the log fire with my following of animals and books, my lamp with its pink shade and my little brown pot for roasting chestnuts, facing the easy chair whose sides were worn by Renaud's arms . . . two springs, already, have opened my entire dark house over a garden ablaze with crimson buds and slender irises with overlong stems. The sunshine drags me out, showers of rain and snow send me firmly back toward the house. But isn't it rather I who decide, with a sigh harassed by the heat, the sudden descent of the clouds swollen with rain, or, with a glance that turns away from the book and the beloved portrait, the return of the sun, the swallow that cleaves the air and the leafless flowering of the crocuses and the white plum trees?

The little dog crouching against my knees shivers. I wake up and feel I've forgotten the time. It's very dark. . . . I've forgotten dinner, it's nearly time to go to sleep . . . come, my animals! Come, discreet little beings who respect my dream! You're hungry. Come with me toward the lamp which reassures you. We're alone, forever. Come! We'll leave the door open so that the night may enter, with its scent of invisible gardenia—and the bat which will hang upside down from the muslin curtains—and he too who does not leave me, who watches over the rest of my life, and for whom I keep my eyelids open, without sleeping, in order to see him more clearly. . . .

Notes

Page

8 In *Claudine en ménage* (Claudine Married), published in
1903, Claudine became infatuated with the beautiful Rézi,
half-Viennese, married to a retired British colonel. Renaud
encouraged this love affair, but Claudine was disillusioned
when she discovered that Rézi was Renaud's mistress.

9 Montigny-en-Fresnois was Caludine's native village, based
on Colette's own Saint-Sauveur en Puisaye, described in
Claudine à l'école (Claudine at School), revisited in later
books in the series, remembered with nostalgia. Luce was a
young schoolgirl who was fond of Claudine; Les Vrimes is
a reference to the place where Claudine's foster sister lived.

In *Claudine s'en va* (Claudine and Annie) Colette de-
scribes a visit to Bayreuth, remembering her own visits
there with her husband Willy soon after their marriage.
Other memories of Bayreuth are described later in *Retreat
from Love*.

Annie Samzun, Claudine's friend, had already appeared

in *Claudine s'en va,* and this novel, subtitled *Annie's Journal* is in fact told by her in the first person.

12 Marcel, Renaud's homosexual son, appeared first in *Claudine à Paris.*

14 Two of Balzac's heroines.

32 Annie's former husband, Alain Samzun, whom she had left (*Claudine s'en va*) on discovering his infidelity.

39 The music critic Maugis first appeared in *Claudine à Paris.* He was "invented" by Willy, but Colette soon learned how to write his curious dialogue. Maugis also appeared in other books written or at least signed by Willy.

Eugène Brieux (1858–1932) was a successful playwright whose plays usually dealt with moral and social problems.

44 Marthe Payet was the sister of Annie's husband, Alain. She appeared in *Claudine à Paris* and the two subsequent books.

53 Calliope van Langendonck, a seductive Cypriot, appeared in *Claudine à Paris* and the two subsequent books.

55 A reference to Balzac's novel, *Le Chef-d'oeuvre inconnu.*

59 La Salpêtrière, a famous Paris hospital originally built in the mid-seventeenth century, now best known for the treatment of mental illness.

61 Michel Provins, contemporary playwright best known for *Les Dégénérés.*

64 Maurice Donnay (1859–1945), a successful playwright of the turn of the century who has been compared to Noel Coward.

The young actress Polaire had successfully played in the stage adaptation of *Claudine à Paris* in 1902.

66 Annie's reference to "young bodies" is reminiscent of the passage in *Mes Apprentissages* (My Apprenticeships) where Colette remembers Polaire's using the same phrase: *la chair fraîche,* literally "fresh" or "young flesh."

67 A reference to the French publishers who had brought out three of the four *Claudine* titles.

73 Old photographs exist showing Colette wearing one of these curious sun hats.

80 A reference to Bostock's Menagerie, originally founded in the early nineteenth century.

91 "Meva" was the assumed name of a contemporary eccentric who wore a long beard and flowing draperies. He also advocated vegetarianism.

100 Alfred Jarry's famous play *Ubu-roi* (1896) had been dedicated to Marcel Schwob, friend of Colette and Willy.

108 A thinly disguised reference to the Théâtre des Mathurins where Colette had played the part of a faun in *L'Amour, le Désir et la Chimère* in 1906.

109 The famous actress Sarah Bernhardt (1845–1923).

115 Colette's caricature of herself as a mime.

118 A reference perhaps to the famous kiss in the mime-drama *Rêve d'Egypte*. When performed by Colette and her friend "Missy," the Marquise de Belboeuf, the scene caused a sensation. *La Retraite sentimentale* was published during the same year (1907).

138 French poet and novelist (1880–1945), who was married for a time to Dr. J.-C.-V. Mardrus, translator of *The Thousand and One Nights* into French. Several of her novels were serialized in *Le Journal*.

Two fashionable contemporary painters.

172 Belle-Île-en-Mer is the largest of the Breton islands, lying about 15 kilometers south of Quiberon. It was here, in 1894, that the young Colette first saw the sea. Sarah Bernhardt built a château here, but it was demolished during World War II, although the old fort where she first lived can still be seen. Le Palais, the port, is the largest town on the island.

173 The Pays des Bigoudens in the southeast of Finistère is named after the curious coiffes worn by the women. The local costumes were famous for their oriental-type embroidery.